A TRAGIC KIND OF WONDERFUL

A TRAGIC KIND OF WONDERFUL

eric lindstrom

POPPY

LITTLE, BROWN AND COMPANY

NEW YORK   BOSTON

Poppy

Hachette Book Group
1290 Avenue of the Americas, New York, NY 10104
Visit our website at lb-teens.com

Poppy is an imprint of Little, Brown and Company.
The Poppy name and logo are trademarks of Hachette Book Group, Inc.

The publisher is not responsible for websites (or their content) that are not owned by the publisher.

First Edition: February 2017

Library of Congress Cataloging-in-Publication Data

Names: Lindstrom, Eric, 1965– author.
Title: A tragic kind of wonderful / Eric Lindstrom.
Description: First Edition. | New York : Little, Brown and Company, 2017. | "Poppy." | Summary: "A sixteen-year-old girl living with bipolar disorder learns to balance romance, friendship, and grief"— Provided by publisher.
Identifiers: LCCN 2016004449 | ISBN 9780316260060 (hardback) | ISBN 9780316260046 (ebook) | ISBN 9780316260039 (library edition ebook)
Subjects: | CYAC: Manic-depressive illness—Fiction. | Grief—Fiction. | Love—Fiction. | BISAC: JUVENILE FICTION / Social Issues / Depression & Mental Illness. | JUVENILE FICTION / Social Issues / Friendship. | JUVENILE FICTION / Family / Siblings. | JUVENILE FICTION / Social Issues / Dating & Sex. | JUVENILE FICTION / Girls & Women. | JUVENILE FICTION / Social Issues / Adolescence.
Classification: LCC PZ7.1.L56 Tr 2017 | DDC [Fic]—dc23
LC record available at https://lccn.loc.gov/2016004449

10 9 8 7 6 5 4 3 2 1

LSC-C

Printed in the United States of America

TO MOM AND DAD,
FOR ALL THE REASONS

ZERO

My big brother, Nolan, used to say everyone has a superpower. Not a skill you learned, but something you were born with. And it's not always cool. Some people get perfect pitch or good intuition, while others get something useless like being able to go a long time without blinking. But if you don't judge, everyone has at least one thing they're really good at.

Nolan's superpower was, quote, "I can make myself be happy."

He proved it by having loud fun with lots of friends most of the time. But it also could be unsettling. Like when he was "happy" at times I knew he shouldn't be. He wasn't faking it exactly. It was real in a way, just not . . . authentic.

Happiness, he said, was like the lights in your house, running on electricity generated by the good things in life. Unhappy people have dark houses without electricity, and they sometimes put candles in their windows to hide their sadness from others, but not Nolan. He said he had a bicycle in his head, attached to an electric generator, and he could imagine pedaling it whenever he wanted to power his real happiness lights.

If you looked closely, though, you could sometimes see his lights dim, or burn too bright, or flicker in ways they weren't supposed to. And once you saw this, you couldn't unsee it. Then you saw it a lot. I didn't understand; I was just a kid at the time. Thinking back on it now, it breaks my heart.

A lot of the time Nolan was naturally happy without having to pedal his imaginary bike. Infectious, too. My happiest memory is from when I was thirteen and he was sixteen, on the first of November.

All of us in Ms. Malik's eighth-grade English class were slumped over our desks like empty puppets, crashed and crumpled after Halloween on a school night. It was silent reading time and we were silent but not reading. If it had been kindergarten naptime, nobody would have complained.

A knuckle cracked. I saw my brother peeking into the room from out in the hall. He waved for me to come over and then ducked away. Maybe something was wrong.

I asked to go to the bathroom, got the nod, grabbed the Magic Wand, and walked into the hall. Nolan was already outside the glass doors at the far end, on his silver eight-speed touring bike. I wondered how he'd managed to slip away from his prison-like high school without being seen.

When I opened the door, Nolan pointed at the Magic Wand. "What the hell is that?"

2

It was really a dowel with a plywood star glued to one end, painted with glitter. It was childish, sexist, and I hated it. The boys used a black dowel with white tips. I hated that, too, though not as much.

I waved it impatiently. "Hall pass. What's wrong?"

"Get on. I'm gonna show you something amazing."

"Now? I can't leave school! Why aren't YOU in school?"

"We won't be gone long. You can say I made you do it. Get on."

"I don't have my helmet."

"Use mine." He held it out.

"Then YOU won't have a helmet."

He rapped his knuckles on his head. "Don't need one."

Classic Nolan. But I knew the risk wasn't getting hurt, it was getting caught, and I wouldn't get in trouble if he didn't wear his helmet. Didn't work the other way. He often got in trouble for stuff I did because Dad said he was "in charge."

I bent over to set the Magic Wand down by the wall—

"No, bring it. We might need it."

I didn't know how that could be possible, but sometimes it was better just to go along when Nolan said random stuff like this.

We rode the trail by the golf course, up and down the gentle slopes. We stopped for smoothies at the Healthee Hut—the sweet strawberry kind with nothing "Healthee" added—and laughed at people drinking bright green blenderized grass. I made him stop at Sandy Park to go on the swings since I knew when he was like this he wouldn't say I was too old and he'd push me super high. I'd shout, "Push me all the way around!" and it always seemed like he really tried to. Next he powered us through the tall weeds in the empty lot to go behind the police station, "So the cops won't see we're cutting school." We stopped at a new store that sold greeting cards and scrapbook supplies and dorky little statues, and it started to get boring till he found a silly joke book that cracked us up. He bought it and off we rode again.

Finally he stopped in front of the bank.

"Ready to see something awesome?"

I'd forgotten that was the point of this trip. Also how I'd been "in the bathroom" at school for over an hour and never showed up to Social Studies.

"What is it?"

"Bring your Magic Wand," Nolan said. He opened the big glass door. "You're gonna love this."

That's where my happiest memory ends.

My own superpower is the ability to not think about anything I don't want to think about. It allows me to relive and enjoy one of the best memories of my life even though it's moments away from my absolute worst.

ONE

Hamster is ACTIVE

Hummingbird is HOVERING

Hammerhead is CRUISING

Hanniganimal is UP!

I'm in a better mood than the situation merits. It's only Thursday, I have tons of homework due tomorrow, we're buried in a long stretch of overcast days, but there's an unexplainable bounce in my step. Well, it's explainable, but I've learned to just enjoy it.

Holly swoops in beside me as everyone streams down the hall toward the exit. I get my usual impulse to touch her storm cloud of kinky black hair. I know she'd be fine with it—other white girls have asked. First she gives them a stern look and says, "How much cash you got?" Then she laughs at their stricken expressions and says, "Sure, whatever, but not for long or it gets weird." I fight the urge anyway. I don't want to be one of those girls.

"Hey, Mel," Holly says. "Want a ride home?"

"Really?" I ask, lighting up. Then I droop. "Oh, darn...I rode my bike today...*and* I'm not going home now...same as *every* day of the *entire year* you've known me."

"Year and four months, if you're counting. I rescued you December of sophomore year."

It's no exaggeration to call it a *rescue*, how she befriended me when I got really sick last year and missed so much school—months, actually—and lost what few friends I had at the time.

She says, "One day you just might find your tires slashed. Then you'll change your tune."

"As if I've been turning down your rides for longer than... what, three days? You got your license Monday?"

"Those tires are so old, I bet I could pop them with a nail file."

"It would make me sad," I say.

"Can't imagine why. That old bike's a P.O.S."

"But it's *my* piece of shit. And a family heirloom. But I meant it'd make me sad if the cops catch you. They'll put you in jail and I'll miss you terribly. You're not supposed to give *any* rides for another...three hundred and sixty-two days."

"Speak for yourself," Declan says, joining us. "*Illegal* isn't the same as *impossible*. I'm tired of walking every day. That's two hours a day wasted. Ten hours a week. Forty—"

I shoot him a look. "It takes you two hours to walk four miles?"

He grins. "I might have added wrong."

"Doubt it. Probably didn't subtract the time you duck behind the library. Though you're right, that *is* part of those two hours a day you're wasting...getting wasted...."

"Baked," he says.

"Tell you what, I'll look up those words in Urban Dictionary if you actually go *inside* the library today and look up the word *hairsplitting*."

Declan snorts. "I'm *grateful* my girlfriend has a license, and a car, *and* a backseat—"

Holly stops his gratitude with an elbow to his ribs. She says to me, "Think of the time *you're* wasting on that bike. I can get you home in no time. Or work, wherever."

"I'm not in a hurry. It's exercise. You should try it. When the apocalypse comes, I'll be ready and you'll be zombie kibble. Come to think of it, you two keep driving everywhere. I don't want to be the slowest in our band of survivors."

When we leave the building, Declan takes a crumpled bag from his pocket.

"Check it out," he says when he sees me looking at it. "I forgot to leave it in the car for the ride home...."

He opens the wrinkled brown sack and shows me a baggie holding what looks like a chunk of sod cut out of someone's lawn.

"Gross." I push it away. "That was in your locker all day? Where'd you even get it?"

His grin gets sheepish. Holly frowns.

"Is that..." I say. "I mean, did your mom make it?"

He nods. "She can't keep track of it all—"

"You're stealing your grandma's *cancer brownies*?"

"Shhh! Tell the world!" He jams the bag under his arm. "She never runs out. My mom always makes more when she runs low."

"That's messed up," I say. "Although...hmmm...let me see it again—"

"No way, Mel. If you want any, you'll have to steal from your own—"

"Declan!" Holly says through clenched teeth, glancing my way.

He stands frozen. My grandma Cece died of stomach cancer a year ago. His comment doesn't upset me, though. Not today.

I tousle his wispy blond hair—there's nothing wrong with touching *his* hair. He hates it but lets me after his blunder. He's not fussy; it just emphasizes how I'm three inches taller than him.

"It's okay, short stuff. I don't need drugs to get high."

Quite the opposite.

———

I say good-bye to Holly and Declan, pop the crossbeam off my U-lock, and stow the pieces in my backpack.

"Mel?"

This is unexpected.

"Hey, Connor."

I'm not sure what else to say. Connor and I aren't friends anymore, though he and I didn't fight like I did with everyone else. We just never spoke again after I was out sick. I focus on strapping my backpack to the rear rack of my bike with a bungee.

"You know what's up with Annie?"

The question is odd enough that I stop what I'm doing to look at him.

It's a normal yet pointless reaction. Connor seldom looks at anyone directly, regardless of whether they're strangers, friends, or ex-friends. Right now he's looking somewhere off to my left. His straight red hair hangs over his forehead.

"She's been sick all week," he says, still not looking at me. "But she won't let us come over. Zumi tried and Annie's mom wouldn't let her in."

Zumi and Annie were the other two friends I lost last year—I only had the three. The fact that he's asking me about them now makes this conversation stranger than anything Annie might be up to.

"And, what, you want my recipe for chicken soup to leave on her porch?"

"She texted us today that she's flying out to see her uncle, I guess the one in Connecticut. That's weird for someone who's been sick a whole week."

"Maybe she's pregnant."

Connor doesn't react to this. "Zumi's really worried about her."

I notice the shield I'm holding up when I feel it start to drop.

He's concerned about Zumi being worried, not about Annie being sick or acting weird. He and I had that in common. Zumi was the best friend I've ever had, and Connor by association. Then Annie and I fought, sides were chosen, and I retreated. I don't blame Zumi or Connor—they had been friends with Annie first, and it was my fault. Though Annie slandering me afterward wasn't.

A car slows to a stop beside us. It's Holly and Declan on their way from the parking lot out to the street.

9

"Everything okay?" Holly asks.

"Yep," I say.

She peers at me, so I smile and wave. "See you tomorrow."

"Call me later." She drives slowly away.

Holly's protective intervention reminds me that while I still miss Zumi and Connor as much as ever, him talking to me now doesn't mean we're suddenly friends again.

"Did Zumi put you up to this?" I say. "Or did you already ask the second-to-last person on earth?"

He glances at me for the briefest possible moment. His wet green eyes look sadder than I remember, but I don't have much to draw from; he's not an eye-contact kind of guy. Some people say it's me, though, that I'm way too much of an eye-contact person.

I say, "You can't really think I've been talking to Annie."

He shrugs. "There's no one else to ask."

I watch Connor walk away toward the parking lot. Someone pushes off from the retaining wall ahead and joins him. It's Zumi: long black hair, pale jeans, and the same black hoodie she was wearing the day I met her.

TWO

The first day of freshman year is hard enough. It's harder start-ing in a new town, like joining a game of musical chairs after the music's already stopped when you don't even want to play. For me, it's even worse than that. I'm still deep in my hole, hardly speaking, a month after moving here, four months after the divorce, and less than a year after losing Nolan.

Despite begging Mom to let me bring my lunch, so I could eat whatever I want and not wait in the cafeteria line, I'm the disap-pointed owner of a lunch card. For more variety of healthier food, according to Mom. I think she's just afraid I'd sit alone outside if I brought my lunch, and I totally would.

On the first day, I get to the cafeteria ahead of most every-one; my previous class and locker are right around the corner. I'm already halfway through my grilled cheese with apple slices—the messy spaghetti was out of the question—before the room starts filling up. Then a group of four girls lines up in front of me.

"This is our table."

She says it without emotion, not snotty or falsely sympathetic. I'm not even worth a sneer. They look like freshmen, too, so they can't possibly have a regular table. There's plenty of room for all of us but I know the score. I grab my tray and scuttle off, silently cursing my mother.

The same girls chase me from a different table the next day. Again I scurry away. This is the next level of harassment. I've been elevated from a random nobody to a specific target.

I hang out in a bathroom stall the third day until I think my oppressors must be sitting down, and then I wait another few minutes, just in case. From the lunch line, I see them at a different table than either of the days before.

As soon as I sit, wondering what Mom would think of the corn dog on my tray, the four girls appear again.

"This is our table."

They actually got up and came over this time.

I start to stand but get stopped by a hand on my shoulder. I look up and see a blond with a French braid beside me.

"Scooch," she says, pushing me sideways hard enough that I instinctively move over.

She plops down and clatters her tray on the table. Another girl sits on my right, close enough that I'm squeezed between them, shoulder to shoulder. All I can see of this other girl is a wall of straight black hair draped down to her black hoodie.

"Oh, I'm sorry," the blond says to the four. "Are we interrupting?"

"It's too sunny here," the tallest harasser says to her friend who'd been talking before. They leave without acknowledging us further, like we'd vanished.

"What's your name?" the blond asks me.

"Mel."

"Like Melody, or Melanie?"

"Just Mel."

"Okay...weird. Anyway, I'm Annie, really Ann, but call me Annie because Ann sounds too...you know. This is Zumi, really Izumi, but call her Zumi. I think it's because she used to zoom around a lot when she was little, and...well..." Annie frowns. "Sometimes she still does. And this..." She twists around and waves impatiently for someone to come over. "This is Connor."

A guy walks over and sits across from us. He doesn't look up from his tray but he seems relaxed.

"The tall one's Gloria Fernandez," Annie says. "The one who does most of the talking is Tina Fernandez, but they're not related. The other two are Elena and Sofia. They're just minions. Gloria's the leader and Tina's her muscle. Like you're my muscle, right, Zumi?"

Zumi turns toward me. Her face is tipped down, but unlike Connor, she looks at me intently, like something creepy from those Japanese horror movies Nolan liked.

"If Team Fernandez ever looks at you again," Zumi says, "tell them you're with us: Annie, Zumi, and Connor. They'll leave you alone."

She says their names all together like a law firm, like how Dad is a part of Jensen, Hannigan, and Hsu. Maybe Zumi's mom or dad's a lawyer, too. Looking around at them, I think they could also be called Sunny, Sullen, and Shy.

Zumi's still scowling. There are big white letters on her sweatshirt, all caps: DON'T ASK. I wonder what it means...but...there's no way to find out. Is that the point, like a joke, or...?

She winks. It's so sudden and unexpected, it makes me laugh. Not Sullen after all.

Zumi points at the untouched corn dog on my tray. "You gonna eat that?"

I wasn't keen on it but the breaded fish option looked worse. And I guess she wants it. Will I have to pay for this new friendship? Or at least the protection? I shake my head and slide the tray toward Zumi.

She shoves it away down the length of the table. "I was just making sure you weren't going to eat it." She smiles. "They taste like shit."

The next day, I wait in the bathroom stall again before lunch. Yesterday seems ages ago and a little unreal. I don't know when Annie, Zumi, and Connor will arrive. Even then, what if they've forgotten all about me?

I carry my tray slowly by them.

"Mel!" Zumi says. She slides over to make room. "We're right here! Sit down!"

For the first twenty minutes, Annie does most of the talking. It's a combination of random bits of everything and filling in basics we didn't cover yesterday. Then she gets an idea.

"Let's ride bikes on the beach trail this Saturday."

I don't want to say no to my first invitation, but my bike

14

rusted out and got left behind in the move. Nolan's bike is fine and parked in the garage, but I've never ridden it alone.

"I don't have a bike."

"Borrow one," Annie says, as if this were obvious. "You have sisters or brothers?"

I shake my head.

"God, you're lucky."

Connor glances up briefly at Zumi and smirks.

Zumi nods slightly. Then she casually says to Annie, "What about your old bike?"

"No, I gave it to Lulu."

"Your mom just got her a new one," Zumi says. "Let's ask her—"

"No, it's . . . it's got a flat tire. We can just walk to the beach; it's fine. I guess you're closest, Mel. We'll meet at your place."

If we end up doing this a lot, they'll probably see Nolan's bike at some point. . . .

"Well, there is a bike in my garage," I say. "It's . . . my cousin's. But it's too big."

"Oh, that's no problem!" Annie says, brightening. "Zumi's brother taught her all about bikes. You're, what, five-seven, five-eight? Probably just need to lower the seat, right, Zumi?"

"I don't know without seeing it," Zumi says to Annie. "But I know I can fix the flat on your old bike."

Connor's shoulders bounce. He's looking at his lasagna, picking at it. I think he's snickering.

"No," Annie says, annoyed. "It's not—" She stops and looks pointedly at Connor. "What?"

He doesn't answer. Zumi leans toward me and says in a low voice, "Lulu's only eleven and Annie's afraid of her."

"I am not," Annie says, more indignant than defensive.

"Okay," Zumi says. "It's just that Annie can't stop Lulu from following her everywhere, so she has to sneak out of the house. She can't do that if we all go over there."

Annie just stares at Zumi like she's waiting for her to finish.

"I can try and adjust your cousin's bike," Zumi says. "Do you want me to?"

I nod.

"Okay, I'll come over before the weekend, in case it takes a while."

"Thanks."

Zumi points a thumb toward Annie and says to me, "But don't you think sneaking around means you're afraid of something?"

I don't think she's really needling Annie; it seems more like affectionate teasing. Annie stares over our heads, looking perturbed.

When I don't answer, Zumi adds, "Maybe just a little?"

Connor laughs.

Annie says, "You be quiet!"

Zumi busts up laughing and I join her.

Team Fernandez walks by, carrying trays back to the kitchen. We instantly stop laughing. Annie coolly eats a bite of lasagna while Connor wrestles with the lid of his juice. Zumi scowls, her head pivoting to keep them in her glare as they walk by, like she's a tracking cannon. The instant they're gone, Zumi giggles, throws her arm around my shoulders, and leans into me hard.

I'm in.

THREE

Hamster is A*CTIVE*

Hummingbird is F*LYING*

Hammerhead is C*RUISING*

Hanniganimal is U*P!*

I'm still in a good mood despite that weird conversation with Connor yesterday. Two days in a row is some kind of record, at least recently. Maybe because it's Friday, and I have almost no homework, and the sun finally came out...but no, I know better. My ups and downs have minds of their own.

I ride after school along the beach trail, pumping the pedals, outpacing the lumbering zombies I imagine chasing me on my way to work. They'll never catch me. Not as long as I have Nolan's bike.

Parked in front of the Silver Sands Suites is a small rental van. Maybe someone's moving in. I head inside. Five minutes later I've locked my stuff in a cabinet by the sink, put on clean scrubs, pinned on my name tag, and washed my face and hands thoroughly.

I check the mirror. Despite vigorous scrubbing, I'm still dotted with freckles. My aunt Joan and I have a long-standing bet that I'll outgrow them. She thinks they're temporary because I have slightly lower density plus brown hair and blue eyes, but I'm less than a month from my seventeenth birthday. As much as I wish she were right, I think I'm going to win this bet…damn it.

In the kitchen I fill a glass of orange juice halfway. I hold it behind my back as I enter the Sun Room. Ms. Arguello is alone here and calls to me, "Excuse me, miss?"

She's in the paisley wingback chair by the south window, knitting a heavy scarf, like every day of the two years I've worked here.

"How's your first day going?" she asks.

"Very well, Ms. Arguello, thank you."

"Oh! You know my name already. How nice, Miss…"

I stoop to bring my name tag closer to her.

"Mel Hannigan?" She laughs. "Was that on your shirt when they gave it to you? Don't worry, I'm sure you'll get your own soon!"

I smile. "No, that's my name."

She looks at me askance, playfully suspicious. "Is it short for Melissa?" I shake my head. "Melinda?"

"Nope, just Mel. What can I do for you?"

I know what she wants—it's the same every day—but she's much happier when I play out this scene naturally.

"Let me know when the mail comes? I'm expecting a letter from my grandson. I'm knitting this muffler for him."

18

"I'll keep an eye out. Is there anything else I can get for you?"

"No, thank you. Or, maybe a small glass of orange juice?"

She smiles when I hand it to her. She doesn't ask why I had it ready. The fact that her letter will never come pops into my head. I push it right back out and leave her to her knitting.

Some days I avoid the Beachfront Lounge for as long as I can, but not today. The Hanniganimal is Up! As soon as I walk in, Mr. Terrance Knight sees me and grins. He sets down his book—today it's his Bible—and struggles out of his usual chair by the heater vent. It's a battle he wants to win without help, and it usually takes a full thirty seconds.

I don't remember how old Mr. Terrance Knight is exactly, but he's at least eighty and still a few inches taller than me, maybe a full six feet. I wait till he's standing and balanced, and then I look up into his eyes, his curly hair shockingly white next to his rich black skin.

"You just get here, Mel? You need to settle first?"

His voice is like thick melted butter; I want to *swim* in that voice. I squint at him and smile with the right side of my mouth. "Mr. Terrance Knight, I'm *never* gonna settle!"

"That's what I want to hear!" he says.

We head for the piano.

My boss's door opens. A wispy ball of white hair like a dandelion pops out—it's Judith.

"Sorry," she says to Mr. Terrance Knight. "I need her."

When I get close, Judith whispers, "Ms. Li. First day. I think she needs some of your magic."

Ms. Li is tiny, sitting in a chair, wearing a simple red silk blouse, black skirt and hose, and pumps that aren't nearly comfortable enough for a woman her age, or any age if you ask me. Her hands are folded in her lap. Tears stream down her wrinkled face.

Standing beside her is a tired middle-aged man, probably a relative, wearing a brown suit that's rumpled and looks slept in.

"This is Mel," Judith says to Ms. Li in a loud voice. "She'll stay with you while we finish up some details. We'll be right outside."

Ms. Li doesn't seem to hear. Judith leads the man out and closes the door.

I sit in the chair next to her. It's good to let them lead.

After another minute of tears and trembling, she looks at me.

I smile. Not my bright smile—I can't imagine she'd want to see that now. I smile in a way that says, *I understand how much the world sucks sometimes . . . but it doesn't always.*

Her eyes crinkle at the corners. I think she heard me.

"Do you want something to drink?" I ask as loud as Judith.

"I'm not deaf," she says. "I just didn't want to answer her endless questions."

"Oh, sorry!" I laugh. "She only wants you to be happy here."

I open the apartment fridge by Judith's desk, retrieve a water bottle, and show it to Ms. Li. She nods. There are plastic cups on the desk; I fill one halfway.

While she sips, I say, "You maybe don't want to hear about how nice this place is, but it's really great. I know it's probably not as good as being at home—"

"Ha! The witch's castle? That's the only good to come of this!"

"What?"

"My daughter-in-law. Wretched woman. I only stayed in her *castle* because of Miles."

"Who's Miles?"

"My other son."

"Is he—"

Her eyes shut and force two more tears down her cheeks.

I take her hand. "I'm sorry. I won't ask any more questions."

She squeezes my fingers and holds on.

"Dad!" a muffled voice says in the hall. "Where is she?"

The door swings open—our hands let go—and someone rushes in and kneels before Ms. Li.

He looks about my age, my height, but nothing else is the same. Everything about him is sharp: his cheekbones, his nose, his chin, his shoulders; even his black hair looks like it's usually neat but now is disheveled and spiky. It reminds me of an angry black cat. I see my hand reaching out to touch—I snatch it back.

The movement catches his eye. He does a double take when he sees my face, caught off guard somehow. He scowls.

"Are you a volunteer?" he asks in a tone that sounds like he's really asking, *Who the hell are you?*

"I work here. I'm—"

21

"You're not a doctor," he says. "Or a nurse. You're just a…
just a…"

He turns back to Ms. Li and grabs her hands.

"Just leave us alone."

I stand and set the water bottle on the desk where they can reach it. Out in the hallway, I look back inside. He's staring at their clasped hands, whispering.

Ms. Li looks up at me with an expression I've seen here many times.

I nod *you're welcome* and close the door.

———

After I leave Ms. Li, I get a text. From Annie. I tap the screen.

**I need to swing by your
house today.**

Bizarre. Must be a mistake. I saw her phone's address book once and there was no one between *Hannigan, Mel* and *Lewis, Connor.* I consider texting Connor about it, but no. They'll figure it out.

An hour later I find Dr. Jordan sitting by a window with a mug of coffee. The direct sun on his face makes it glow almost as white as his hair.

I sit across from him. "Hey."

He's a resident and wants me to call him Piers. It feels too weird, though, so I rarely call him anything directly. He's a retired psychiatrist but won't let me call him Dr. Jordan because he's not my real doctor. Except he kind of is.

"How are you today?" he says.

"Are you asking, or are you *asking*? If you're *asking*, I'm not a danger to myself or others."

Dr. Jordan watches me over his coffee, amused.

"What?" I say.

"I do so enjoy our time together. You're like the daughter I never had."

"Granddaughter."

He salutes me with his mug.

None of the other ears nearby work very well. I'm free to talk.

"I think my meds need a little adjusting."

"Feeling mixed? For how long?"

"Today. Right now, at least. I don't know. I'm revving up but also losing energy."

"An off day isn't a cocktail issue. Anything stressing you out at school, or with friends?"

"No. Maybe. I don't know. I don't *want* it to be about any of those things. That should count for something."

He sips his coffee.

"I know," I say. "I can't choose how I feel, but I can choose how I think about how I feel."

"That's not quite what I said, although I suppose it's an adequate enough street version."

I sneer.

"Seriously," he says. "You need to talk to your doctor. About everything. Not just the meds. I'm not—"

"Not my doctor, *I know*."

"I was going to say I'm not going to be around forever."

23

He watches me. Usually it's other people who get uncomfortable with how much I hold eye contact. Now I get a glimpse of how they feel.

"I'm glad you didn't," I say and stand up. "That would've been a shitty thing to say."

In the two years I've worked here, first as a volunteer and now as an employee, I've seen half a dozen residents leave the permanent way—through the roof, as Judith says—including Grandma Cece. I miss her, of course, and all the others who've left through the roof, but I really don't know what I'd do without Dr. Jordan.

I sit back down.

"Sorry."

"You've come a long way, Mel. And in a very short time."

"Thanks to you."

"In *spite* of me. I promised Cece I'd help with life coaching, but we talk so much, it relieves the emotional pressure to engage with your therapist. More proof I was right to give up my practice. If I were doing this properly, I wouldn't let sentiment and a promise to Cece stop me from cutting you off, to push you into a more productive relationship with your doctor. I shouldn't be—"

"Your 'life coaching' *saved me*, Dr. Jordan. I'm sorry if you *regret* that—"

His look stops me. It's a subtle expression but I know it.

"I mean…my *real* doctor thought your *life coaching* was wrong! I wrote down his exact words…." I get my phone and thumb open the notebook app. "He said I was *fetishizing the*

24

personification of my symptoms. He also said my *bipolar disorder couldn't be cycling as fast as I claimed, not at my age*."

Dr. Jordan's eyes narrow. "He *thought* it was wrong? Don't you mean he *thinks* it's wrong?"

Oops.

"I mean back when we talked about it," I say.

"You never told me."

"You just said I talk to you too much! And there's plenty I don't tell you! He said I should stop talking to you so I stopped talking to him!"

Dr. Jordan sips his coffee. He once made the mistake of telling me Winston Churchill would relight his cigar to give him time to think or compose pithy, articulate statements. Now I know what Dr. Jordan's coffee is really for.

"I thought you said something last week about your doctor being a woman."

Shit. "Yeah. That other guy moved away. My new doctor, she just wants me to fill out questionnaires and talk about the meds. As long as I say I'm fine, I'm out the door."

"So you haven't given her a chance."

"I answer all her questions."

"Mel, some doctors push you and divine meaning from what you say when pushed. Others wait to hear what you say on your own and divine meaning from what you offer up. Offer something up. Give her a chance."

I don't say anything.

Dr. Jordan sets his mug down. "Tell her what's going on in your life. And if you feel strongly about something, say so.

Stand your ground; defend your feelings. Be honest and hold nothing back. A good therapist will help you understand and process, not argue. Try her out this afternoon and see. It can only help."

Hold nothing back? How could I possibly tell that quiet woman in her sterile little office things I'm not willing to tell Dr. Jordan? Things I don't even let cross my own mind? It's inconceivable.

FOUR

Hamster is *Running*

Hummingbird is *Perched*

Hammerhead is *Cruising*

Hanniganimal is *Level / Mixed*

Dr. Oswald doesn't seem old enough to be a psychiatrist. She's slim, with dark skin, nice bone structure in her face, and wearing a stylish off-white sweater, like an eggshell, with navy slacks. None of the young psychiatrists I've seen were any good. I mean to talk to. They've been okay about tuning my meds.

She sits there with this nice, open expression, ready for me to...what? I don't know. And the stress of not knowing, plus maybe telling her about the Hanniganimal today, has shifted my moods even faster than usual. This is our third session and the office is less empty this time. The shelves have more books. There are more framed diplomas on the wall, a Van Gogh print of birds over a field, a bonsai tree on her desk with a tiny origami crane in its branches—

"It seems like something's on your mind," she says. "We have some time left."

We'd talked about the routine stuff after I filled out the long weekly questionnaire: Manic Episodes? (no), Depression? (the usual amount), Irritability? (no), Rage? (no), Sleeplessness? (nothing I can't handle), Obsessive Thoughts? (they mostly mean about sex, and *no*), Suicidal Thoughts? (definitely not, and that should be the first question), and so on.

Annie called right before my appointment—couldn't be a mistake this time, not with my name and picture popping up on her screen—and my mind started racing as I declined it. She left no message and that made it even worse. I'm not going to mention tweaking my meds.

"Want to talk about it?" she says. "Or anything else?"

No. Yet I also don't want to say *no* tomorrow when Dr. Jordan asks if I gave her a chance. I swung by the house on my way here to bring my charts, but I'm getting cold feet.

"You're the doctor," I say. "What should we talk about? My meds are working pretty well. No one at school even knows there's anything wrong with me."

"You *are* doing very well, way above average for someone with your symptoms. Mainly because you aren't resistant to medication. That's a lot of the battle right there."

"I don't feel like I'm winning anything."

"Battles are never won. Only survived."

"Then what's to talk about? There's no cure. I'm as good as I'm going to get."

"Dr. Fletcher wrote in his notes about things you haven't told your friends, to protect yourself. Some trigger topics—"

28

I stiffen and she raises a hand.

"I won't bring them up with only a few minutes left today. But you have painful, *real* emotions, which aren't symptoms. Talking about them will make you feel better."

I don't say anything.

"I'll give you a stack of blank forms so you can fill them out before you arrive. That way we can spend our time talking instead of you filling them out here. Okay?"

Has she guessed that I fill them out slowly on her sofa to use up time?

"You're saying next week I have to talk about…"

"*No*. You don't have to talk about anything you don't want to."

I watch her carefully.

"It's okay, Mel. Dr. Fletcher had…an aggressive style of talk therapy. That's not how I work. We can just talk about the weather every week till you go off to college if you want. But I do want us to talk. Okay?"

Dr. Oswald gives me a real smile, not some obvious bull-shit psychiatrist version.

I want to believe her. Only it wasn't just Dr. Fletcher. Every doctor except Dr. Jordan has pushed me, or thought I was exaggerating my symptoms, or both.

"So…" she says, "I came from Seattle. Does it ever rain here?"

I smile. "Not much."

"That's a shame. I like the rain. Do you?"

I'm relieved. And grateful. Maybe I can try this after all.

I take a deep breath. "When my parents divorced three years ago, six months after…you know…what happened with my brother...I was pretty messed up. We moved here and then a year and a half later, I...had my breakdown. Grandma Cece was friends with a psychiatrist living on the same floor of her retirement home, Dr. Jordan, and...well, he won't talk about my meds—he's retired and won't be my *real* doctor—but he taught me things that pretty much saved me."

"You were thinking about hurting yourself?"

"God, no, nothing like that. But my dad says there's lots of ways to ruin your life."

"How did Dr. Jordan help you?"

"Too many ways to tell you in just a few minutes, but..."

I pull the printouts from my pocket and unfold them. These graphs are my life decoded; I'm not keen on showing them to anyone. They're like pages from my diary, or poems I wrote from the deepest, most secret place in my heart, the kind other people would think are silly. I hand them over.

"He taught me that bipolar disorder doesn't just mean bouncing between manic and depressed. That my rapid cycling isn't just doing it faster than most. That my mixed states aren't just being depressed and manic at the same time. He showed me it's all much more complicated than that, but also how to break it down."

She looks at my graphs and sits up straighter.

"I'm a mix of all these forces. We talked about it like they were all different animals."

Dr. Oswald looks at me thoughtfully. I don't know what her expression means. It doesn't seem negative.

"The Hamster is my Head, for how clear my thinking is.

When my Hamster is Running or Sprinting in its wheel, I'm sharp or racing. If it's Stumbling, I can still think fast but I'm muddled and can't put two thoughts together, or I can't stop thinking something over and over. The attention-deficit part."

She's listening. So far so good.

"The Hummingbird is my Heart, how much energy I have. When my Hummingbird is Flying, I want to run around, or if it's Speeding I stay up for days without sleeping. If it's Perched or Asleep, I want to lie down."

She's not judging. Not yet, anyway.

"The Hammerhead is my physical Health. Cruising when I'm fine; Slogging or Thrashing if I'm sick. And I'm the Host, which is my mood generally plus the combination of the other animals. What Dr. Jordan and I started calling the Hanniganimal—"

"I'm sorry, the … ?"

"The Hannigan Animal. The HANN-i-GAN-i-mal. Me."

My voice is getting quiet but I keep going. If this time goes bad like the others, I don't want it to be my fault because I half-assed it.

"My animals have minds of their own. They go up and down separately. When they're all down at the same time, I'm depressed. When they're all up together, I'm manic. Other times I'm Mixed. Like when the Hanniganimal is Down but my Hamster and Hummingbird are Running and Flying, I feel a dark, gloomy, anxious kind of manic energy."

"Dysphoric mania," Dr. Oswald says.

"Yeah, I guess. Anyway, I record everything a few times

a day to make these graphs, or more often if I'm cycling rapidly enough. Seeing everything separated out helps me keep it together."

Dr. Oswald examines my charts, pressing her palm down on the creases.

"Everything starts with H...." she says. "Head Hamster, Heart Hummingbird, Health Hammerhead, Hannigan the Host..." She looks up. "The Hanniganimal."

She's trying to hide her expression, the way Dr. Jordan relaxes his face to not show judgment, except she's not quite succeeding. My alarms aren't going off, though. I try to keep my paranoia from revving up.

"Is that why you chose a Hammerhead for Health? Because it starts with *H*? All your other animals seem to more closely match what they represent."

"Oh..." I wince. "Not exactly. My Hammerhead is how good my body feels, not just whether I've caught a cold or something. Look back a couple weeks, where my Hammerhead was Slogging? I wasn't actually sick. Those days with the red asterisks?"

Her eyes widen.

"Yeah. Shark Week."

Her hand flies to her mouth.

Is she...?

"Are you laughing?"

She looks at me. Her eyes are reflecting more light. Not sparkling, just shinier.

"No, Mel. I'm not laughing. These charts, they're very special."

32

"You're making fun of me."

"No, I mean it. This is wonderful. Truly. Thank you."

"Uh, you're welcome? For what? It's not a Mother's Day card."

"I understand this was difficult for you to share. I'm very glad you did. It's remarkable. And it's something we can really talk about. When we're not talking about the weather."

I relax and sit back.

"Dr. Jordan sounds like a smart guy," she says. "If you're keeping your diagnosis secret, how did you come to tell him?"

"*He* told *me*. Well, he told Grandma Cece, then she told my mom. It's in the family—my aunt Joan and my brother—and he said it was a dead giveaway when I talked to him for twenty minutes in one long rambling sentence."

"Pressured speech."

"Yeah. There are boring names for everything."

"There certainly are. These charts are much more interesting."

"Do they help you? So you can tell me...I don't know... how to get better?"

"Is that what you've been waiting for? For me to tell you what to do?"

Not exactly. I was mostly trying to run out the clock. But now...

"I only need prescription refills every month or two. Why else do I need to come every week?"

"To give you a safe place to talk." She waves at her diplomas. "I went to school to study how to prescribe medication,

33

but also to learn good questions to ask, questions you might not think to ask yourself. But only you can answer them."

I slump. "Why can't you be like psychiatrists in the movies? You know, confront me with truths I don't want to face, explain the hidden root of my problems, tell me how to fix everything if I were brave enough?"

"I thought you didn't like Dr. Fletcher's approach."

"Oh, when you put it that way..."

"Do you wish your life were like a movie?"

"Only if it's a good movie. Doesn't everyone?"

"What *you* think is all that matters here. What do *you* want?"

I think a moment. "Maybe a nice musical."

Dr. Oswald smiles.

Something else occurs to me. "Actually, I want to tell Dr. Jordan to invite you over for poker night."

Dr. Oswald laughs. "I have a bad poker face?"

I grin. Comfortable for the first time in any doctor's office.

Except now I'm worried about what I might tell her next week.

FIVE

It's Saturday and Annie's up in Napa Valley with her family. I want to hang out with Zumi and Connor but I've never called them directly before. In the few weeks since we met, Annie's been the center of everything. I hope that's not part of the deal. She's not stand-offish exactly...well, sometimes...but it often seems like she wishes she were with other people. I mostly just don't want Zumi to think I only want to be friends with Annie, not when it's really Zumi and Connor I like, but I can't bring myself to pick up the phone—

Zumi texts me:

Awake?

I exhale.

Yep. You? Ha ha.

Can I come over?

Sure. Where's Connor?

Probably home. C u soon.

While I wait in the living room for Zumi to pedal over, Mom leaves to go buy the weekly groceries. Not long after, I hear a squeal from the front of the house—tires on the driveway from someone braking too hard. Must be Aunt Joan rolling in from wherever she spent the night.

Six feet tall, stick thin, ginger, pasty, spotted, graceful as a giraffe walking backward, that's Mom's little sister, HJ—short for Hurricane Joan. She calls herself the redheaded stepchild but my own freckles prove the genes are in our family tree. The door opens hard enough to bounce off the wall, possibly adding another dent; keys jangle, she kicks the entry table, brushes the pedal of my bike, drops what sounds like her work binders, or her cavernous purse, or both, and mutters "Shit!" three or four times.

Her Saturday moods depend on when she comes home from being out Friday night. This morning she seems pretty upbeat and starts rooting around in the fridge, so wherever she was didn't include breakfast but didn't leave her in a sour mood.

A minute later, Zumi pounds on the front door. I know it's her because she uses the side of her fist instead of knuckles. It's new to HJ, though.

"What the hell? Jehovah's Witnesses getting more aggressive?"

"No, it's—" I crack my shin on the coffee table trying to run around it. "Ow, shit!"

36

"It's okay, I'll get it. I'm in the mood for a fun argument." HJ opens the door.

"Oh," she says. "You don't look like you're here to talk about Jesus. Unless you're hiding a Bible behind your back. You here for Mel?"

"Yeah," Zumi says. "You're not her. Unless you got taller and older since yesterday."

"Older?" HJ raises her eyebrows. "How old do you think I am?"

"No, Zumi, don't!" I say, rubbing my throbbing shin.

Zumi squints. "Twenty-nine?"

HJ squints back. "Honest answer?"

Zumi winces. "Not really?"

HJ sighs and steps aside for Zumi to come in. "What kind of name is Zumi anyway? Sounds Aztec or Mayan."

"Do I look like I'm from Mexico?"

"You look like you're from Japan but I bet you aren't."

Zumi smiles. "I was born a couple miles from here. On the kitchen table, supposedly. I'm still not sure if it's a true story or just something my brother wants me to believe and my parents keep playing along."

I laugh. I think if Annie were here, she'd have said, "Zumi, gross!" with a look of genuine disgust. She wouldn't have laughed. But then again, if Annie were here, Zumi wouldn't have said it.

"Zumi," I say. "This is my aunt Joan."

"Call me HJ." She walks back to the kitchen.

"I like her," Zumi says, not whispering. "Where can I get one?"

"Be careful what you wish for."

We spend the next couple hours sitting in my room, talking and laughing. *I keep expecting her to stand up and say it's time to go, or call Connor, but she doesn't. She stays for lunch—Frankenstein sandwiches we make from random stuff in the fridge—and then we're back in my bedroom.*

"Hey," Zumi says. "Is that what I think it is?"

My closet door is ajar and she pulls it all the way open. She grabs a box. Oh no . . .

"Why do you have a karaoke machine in here?"

"Because . . . my aunt was a very different kind of teenager? And she can't understand that? And she keeps trying to fix me?"

"It's never been opened."

"I keep meaning to return it. I guess it's too late, now. You can have it if you want."

"Already got one. Let's go!" *She's out the door.*

I find Zumi in the living room behind the TV. The karaoke box is torn open on the floor.

"What are you doing?"

"Looking for pirate treasure. Oh wait, I already found some. I just need to plug it in. . . ."

Against my silent hope, Zumi gets it working in less than two minutes. She thumbs through the screen menu with the remote. "No songs from this century? So much Madonna, my mom would love it, but God, if I hear 'Borderline' one more time . . . See anything you want to sing?"

I don't answer.

"Here's some less ancient stuff . . . not bad . . . something for everyone. What's first?"

"You," *I say.* "You first."

"Okay," Zumi says.

I regret my word choice. The clear implication is that I'll go second.

The screen scrolls to LADY GAGA *and stops on "Bad Romance."*

It starts, blaring at high volume, but Zumi doesn't soften it. The first lyrics on the screen aren't words, just chanting, and she dives right in. She's done this before. Not just karaoke; this exact song.

I glance out through the dining room and see Mom and HJ standing outside the glass door, staring in, drawn by the commotion. It looks like they were eating lunch at the backyard picnic table.

Zumi belts out the song like her life depends on it, rocking left and right. She even stretches her arm out to point at the imaginary audience behind the TV.

It's loud and shocking, and she sings so fluidly without stumbling, it takes a moment to register that her voice is . . . off. I don't know anything about singing, but I understand it requires skill beyond saying the right words at the right times. Zumi lacks this skill.

She spins around and points at me, singing without needing to watch the screen. I see it on her face, behind the grin she's fighting to suppress. She knows she's a lousy singer.

I cover my face—I can't let her see what I'm thinking. She laughs and spins around again, singing louder now.

It's glorious.

The sliding glass door to the backyard opens. HJ walks in and Mom slowly slides the door closed again, watching from outside where it's safe.

Zumi sees HJ bobbing to the music and waves her in. HJ doesn't pretend to be reluctant. I've heard her sing lots of times—in the shower, the car, or randomly when she's flying high—and I know they're well matched in their lack of talent. Like me, if I had the guts to stand up and open my mouth.

By the time the song ends, I'm laughing at the both of them. They shake hands, exaggerating like their arms are wet noodles.

"It's a pleasure to sing with someone as bad as me," HJ says. "Thank you very much!"

Zumi laughs. "No one ever thanks me for singing!"

I grin. Then I stop. HJ's holding out the microphone to me.

They both laugh as if something on my face is suddenly hilarious.

Zumi takes pity and says they'll be my training wheels. They prop me up between them and we sing the next song on the list, "Poker Face," without either of them calling me out on how I'm silently lip-synching.

"Gimme!" HJ grabs the remote. She scrolls up the list. "Aha! I had lots of machines to choose from, but only one at the store had this...."

She stops scrolling at ABBA: *"Take a Chance on Me."*

"Okay," HJ says. "This time with feeling."

"And volume," Zumi whispers in my ear.

Mom steps up. I didn't hear her come inside. She smiles. "Ready?"

I'm not, but by late afternoon, I'm singing audibly, then loudly, even dancing some. I prove to others what I already knew, that in addition to being a bad singer, I'm also a terrible dancer.

Zumi texts Connor to come over. He does, but he just watches and won't leave the sofa. Whenever we try to drag him up, he closes his eyes and goes limp till we give up. An hour later, all our phones buzz at the same time. It's a group text from Annie:

Home. Come over.

"*Let's go!*" *Zumi runs to retrieve her hoodie from where she'd flung it behind the sofa.*

I start to pack up the machine and Mom says, "You're not taking that, are you? It's too big for your bike."

"*No," Zumi says. "Annie hates stuff like karaoke."*

"*I'll put it away," HJ says. "You guys go and have fun."*

Now I guess we'll go listen to Annie talk about Napa. I feel a pang watching Zumi scurry with excitement for Annie's return. I get the feeling, not for the first time, that Zumi might want to be more than Annie's best friend.

"*Text me if you want to stay out late," Mom says and heads for her room. I hear the door close. Ever since we lost Nolan, on the rare occasions where Mom has fun, she disappears into her room for a while afterward to pay for it.*

I often do, too. Not this time, though. Nolan would want me to keep the party going.

SIX

Hamster is *RUNNING*

Hummingbird is *PERCHED*

Hammerhead is *CRUISING*

Hanniganimal is *LEVEL / MIXED*

It's dusk by the time I get home from Dr. Oswald's office. Dad's Mercedes is parked on the street. There's plenty of room in the driveway next to Mom's old Toyota but he and Mom aren't together so their cars shouldn't be together. Dad doesn't like mixed messages. He hasn't accepted that we've stopped listening to his messages, mixed or otherwise.

I open the front door and wheel my bike inside. I clatter more than necessary. Dad's sitting at the kitchen table, probably wincing.

While I free my backpack from its bungee and take off my shoes and socks, I imagine a conversation we stopped repeating long ago, the one where he tells me bikes belong in the garage. I say it's too much hassle. He says it's more important to do things right. I ask him, what makes it *right*?

It's an argument he can't win—it's not logical. He's tried that route, too:

The tires are dirty because they touch the road (so do my shoes)....

The rubber marks the wood floor (so do my shoes)....

I shouldn't wear shoes inside, either (I couldn't give a shit and neither could Mom)....

I don't think everything that happened with Nolan caused the divorce. Mom and Dad were shaky for years before it all blew up. It really came down to Dad thinking there were all kinds of rules about everything. Like you were supposed to wear socks in the house because shoes would scratch the wood floor, but skin oil from bare feet would ruin the finish (maybe in a thousand years). Mom and I couldn't remember all this stuff, let alone do it right. Dad said there was no need to memorize anything because it was all *intuitively obvious.*

Not to us, so Dad left to find his true tribe. He's still looking. We couldn't afford to keep the house, even with alimony and child support on the first of every month without fail. I didn't want to stay anyway. I'd withdrawn from everyone and everything by that point and was surrounded by bad memories. Even superpowers have limits.

As soon as I finished middle school, Mom and I moved a hundred miles across the bay here to Costa Vista, south of San Francisco, to the house where Mom grew up with its deeply scratched wood floors. Grandma Cece had previously moved into the Silver Sands Suites and was letting Aunt Joan live here rent-free.

Mom stirs two pots at the same time in the kitchen. She's already changed out of work clothes and into baggy overalls, her thick auburn hair pulled back in a sloppy ponytail. We wave to each other and I drop my backpack hard on the dining room table. Dad's mouth tightens.

"I'm not packed," I say, though weekend packing takes five minutes max. "I thought you were coming tomorrow."

"Sorry, I can't." He shakes his head. "I have to go to Monterey. Partners are flying up from LA."

"I could go to the aquarium."

"I'll be busy from morning into the night both days."

"That's what the aquarium's for."

"Sorry, not this trip."

I'm sorry, too. I can tell he means it, but I think if he really knew me, the fact that I wasn't serious about the aquarium would be *intuitively obvious*.

"How's school?"

I give him enough fuel to keep the conversation running. I know his motivational technique; he doesn't express direct disappointment. He just sets the bar ten percent higher than wherever I am. I'm a solid B student, but if I got all As, I'd hear the same speeches about trying harder, applying myself more, taking my future seriously. In Dad's world, potential is like a rainbow, this beautiful thing you should chase even though it always stays out of reach.

He leaves me and Mom to our penne with generic-brand marinara sauce and garlic bread that's really toasted sandwich bread with butter and garlic salt. It's what sent him on his way tonight. Not seeing what we were reduced to eating, but that it's one of our favorite meals.

"Were his golf clubs in the car?" I ask Mom while we clear the dishes. "Monterey means Pebble Beach."

"That's really how they have meetings, you know."

"Sounds like a wonderful life."

Tires screech on the driveway. Time to brace for Hurricane Joan.

I wish Dad were still here for this.

———

I sit on the toilet lid, toes on the floor, bouncing my legs—my energy coming back—as I watch HJ lean into the mirror over the sink. She applies eyeliner fast enough to twist my gut, worried she'll jab her eye.

Mom passes the bathroom door. "Joanie, if you use all the Q-tips, pick up some more while you're out." I know that's never going to happen. Maybe Mom realizes this too, since she adds, "Or at least write it on the list."

"Yes, *Patricia.*..." HJ tosses the eyeliner on a shelf, picks up a naked mascara wand, and knocks clutter around till she finds the tube. "Mel, please tell me you've got a date tonight. A pretty girl like you, it's a waste to spend Friday night in this rat hole."

"But it's *our* rat hole."

She starts in with the mascara. "Until Pats kicks me out. I'm a bad influence."

45

"That's not what Dad calls you—"

She laughs—it's like a bark. "I'll bet!"

"He says you're an inappropriate role model."

"He thinks I'm a role model? That's sweet. Don't change the subject. It's Date Night!"

"You go out every night—"

"I mean for you, you're in school—don't distract me. Tonight is Date Night. If you don't have one, get one. That's *my* plan."

"I have a date tonight."

She stops to look at me, eyebrows raised.

"With my soul mate...*Netflix*."

She grimaces. "I've failed as an inappropriate role model."

My phone rings. Curious. Usually only Mom or Dad calls out of the blue.

It's Annie again. I decline it again. Not going to think about that, not on a Friday night.

"Who was that?"

"Nobody. Wrong number."

"If it's an unknown number, maybe it's a new guy from school calling. How can you know without answering?"

"I'm psychic."

HJ finishes her eyes and grabs a different eyeliner pencil. This is my favorite part. She hates her freckles—or, quote, her "blotchy face"—except she has a bare patch under her left cheekbone the size of a dime. She draws fake freckles on it to blend it in. It's both wonderful and tragic.

My phone burps.

"You've *got* to change that ringtone."

"That's what Holly would say if she knew I assigned it to her." I tap the screen to read her text.

Busy?

"You're popular tonight," HJ says. "Is it a boy?"
"I don't know any *boys*."
I text back:

Kinda.

Burp:

Important?

With Hurricane Joan.
Almost done. What's up?

Burp:

Movie Roulette. You in?

"Please, Mel. It's disgusting."
I switch it to vibrate and then text:

Not sure I feel like being a
third wheel tonight.

**We want you to come.
Bring someone if you
want. Or we can find you
someone! ;)**

Ha! Don't you dare. I'll go if
it's just us three. We'll need
a ride.

47

Got it covered. :)

I sigh.

I'm not bringing bail money.

See you in twenty.

"There," I say to HJ. "Happy? I'm going out with friends. Friday Night Binge with my One True Love is postponed."

"Just friends, huh? It's a start." She stands tall and faces me, head cocked to the left, chin up—she knows her good angles. "Verdict?"

I smile. "Amazing. The world is not prepared."

"Damn right, it's not. I'm going to reel in a good one tonight, you'll see."

I gesture vaguely. "Especially if you go out in just the bra and panties."

She puts her hands on her hips and winks. "Plan B."

As we head out of the bathroom, my phone vibrates again. A text from Annie this time.

You home? I'm out front.

Huh? I open the door and peek out. A gleaming white car, something fancy, is parked facing the wrong way at the curb. I see silhouettes of people behind tinted windows.

The car's front passenger door opens. Annie appears.

Her sense of style has grown up some but still includes buttoned collared shirts and the French braid she's always worn.

She says, "You didn't call me back."

48

Does she think her disappointed tone means something to me? Or does she not even know she does it?

My heart's pounding anyway. Not from her tone, but from her being here at all. It can't be good. She walks to the trunk as it slowly opens with a hiss.

I step out onto the porch. "What do you want?"

Annie picks up a cardboard box the size of a microwave, and then she closes the trunk gracefully with one hand. She walks along the sidewalk and up to meet me without cutting across the grass. She doesn't look remotely sick. She looks done up—beautiful, even. But supposedly so was Lucifer.

"I have something to give you before we leave town."

"To Connecticut?"

I'm not sure why I feel the need to tell her I know this. I've never liked how competitive she is, or how competitive I sometimes became when around her.

"Paris." She smiles.

She doesn't sound sarcastic. It seems like one of her self-important pronouncements.

"Why'd you tell Zumi and Connor you were going to your uncle's?"

"We are, until we find our own place. He lives in Paris now."

"Your own place? You're not coming back?"

Annie holds out the box. "Here."

I cross my arms. "What's in it?"

"Mostly Zumi's stuff. Some of Connor's."

A loud hum from the car makes me jump. The driver's window lowers two inches.

"Annie," her mom says impatiently.

49

The window slides closed again. The skin down my neck and back tightens.

Annie rattles the box. "Are you going to take this?"

"Why don't *you* give it to them?"

She sighs and sets it down on the porch.

I get it. Annie lied about being sick to keep Zumi and Connor away, so they wouldn't see her family packing. It strikes me that Annie and I have both lied to them about being sick in order to hide something.

I say, "You're not going to tell Zumi?"

Annie's eyes roll. It's genuine and crude—not one of her poised, choreographed looks. Then she walks backward toward the car and points at the box. "She can sort out what's hers and what's Connor's."

Something about this doesn't add up.

I drop my arms. "Why didn't you just mail this?"

"I thought you and I could be friends again someday. When we grew up. After everything blew over. Maybe we still can?"

She looks for something in my eyes. Whatever it is, she's not going to find it. I'm not her minion anymore. I wouldn't follow her if I was lost and she knew the way to heaven.

"Guess it wasn't meant to be," she says, pouting her lips. It almost seems sincere. Then she shrugs. "C'est la vie."

"So..." I say, trying to wrap my head around this. "You're just leaving?"

Annie cocks her head. "Already sold the house." She pats the hood of the car. "And the Beamer. All we have to do is drop it off. Plane leaves in three hours."

"You have to at least say good-bye—"

"I *am* saying good-bye—"

"To someone who cares. You…" I swallow. "You know how Zumi feels about you."

Annie shrugs. "I know how I feel about her."

I clench my fists. "God, you're unbelievable. What would it cost you to tell her you're sorry you have to go?"

"Wow, Mel…it's been a while since I've seen you this worked up. Don't waste it trying to protect someone you're not friends with anymore. Someone who hates you."

Annie opens the car door.

I step down off the porch. "You really came here thinking…what? That I'd want to see you again? You don't care about anybody. At least now Zumi will finally believe it."

"She'll get over it. You did. Au revoir."

The instant she closes the door, the car accelerates away and turns the corner without slowing at the stop sign.

I sit down hard on the porch next to the box. I can't look at it.

Ten minutes later the front door opens.

"Mel?" HJ says. "Something wrong?"

Only that I gave away Zumi, my best friend, to someone she wanted more, walked away, watched the bridges burn, and now it was all for nothing.

"Mel?"

I can't explain it. Even if I wanted to, I wouldn't know where to begin.

SEVEN

Hamster is *Running*

Hummingbird is *Flying*

Hammerhead is *Cruising*

Hanniganimal is *Down / Mixed*

Midway through the movie I look around again. I can't say there's not a dry eye in the house since only half of them are dripping. The rest are dry and distant, from rolling or from thousand-mile stares. Declan is slouched so far down I doubt his butt is on the seat cushion. Holly never slouches and her expression is less slack-jawed, but she's restless like when she's bored and trapped.

They'd pulled into the driveway while HJ was trying to get me to talk—I'd completely forgotten they were coming. I ran the box inside, hid it in my closet, ran back out, and tried to act like nothing happened. I didn't feel like Movie Roulette anymore but couldn't cancel now without explanations I wasn't willing to give.

I hoped the movie might stop the conversation with Annie from looping in my head. It's too fresh to block out on my own.

Trying not to think about it, and failing, is winding me up more and more. Every few minutes Holly touches my knee to tell me to stop bouncing my legs; I don't even know I'm doing it until she does and then I stop, but a few minutes later it happens again. Unfortunately the movie isn't enough to distract me. Worse, it's not just boring, it's aggravating.

If I remember the novel correctly, which I do, and if they didn't change it much, and they haven't yet, we're coming to a part that's going to be longish, quietish, and unbearable without any *ish* whatsoever.

I can't take it much longer, this sappy nonsense playing out on the big screen in front of us. Somebody has to do something about it. For everyone's sake. But no one will. It's up to me.

I scrunch down and cup my hands around my mouth....

"In a world..."

Holly's head whips around.

"...of sobbing twelve-year-old girls..."

People laugh and heads turn. I'm definitely not the only one. It's not just guys laughing, either. Being immune to this Kool-Aid is an equal-opportunity agony.

"...based on the book that changed your life forever...in the seventh grade..."

Declan laughs. Holly swats my leg and hisses, "Stop it!" but I can't stop now....

"...comes a movie about a love so strong it defies believability, reason, the ability to digest solid food...."

"Quiet!" someone yells up front. Tearful. Definitely no older than thirteen.

I'm unmoved. These people need to know life's nothing like what's on this screen. Besides, too many people are laughing now, pent up from silently enduring an hour of this feature-length Hallmark commercial. They get it.

"And the guy's a pussy!" some dude in the back shouts. His friends shush him but they're laughing, too.

"Shut up!" another crying girl yells. She can't be more than ten. I guess some people's lives were changed in elementary school. "He's going to *die* for her!"

"Spoiler!" someone yells, laughing.

"Snape kills Dumbledore!"

"Shut *UP!*"

Roars of laughter and a room divided. Holly covers her eyes with one hand.

I press on. "The story of a girl pursued by a dreamboat she doesn't love whose *sole purpose* is to *die* for her...with a smudge of dirt on his cheek and perfect hair..."

"Be *quiet!*"

"*Don't* be quiet!" More laughter.

The room's in chaos, the laughing faction joking loudly, the sobbing sisterhood whispering indignantly. A woman storms the exit. No way she's alone. She's a mom with her kids, her daughters—at least I really hope so—and she's going to tattle.

"See you outside," I whisper and head for the aisle, crouching low.

"You're not leaving me here," Declan says.

Holly comes, too. Cheers and jeers follow as we walk quickly up the aisle. We pass behind the mom who's bitching out some poor guy who only knows how to scoop cold stale popcorn into thin cardboard boxes.

We escape into the cool night air. They're laughing. I'm not.

Holly says, "That was mean."

"Then stop giggling," Declan says.

"I'm not *giggling*. And I didn't say it wasn't funny. I guess I'm a bad person."

"Not as bad as Mel!" He holds his arms up to protect Holly from me. "I think we need to call an exorcist!" He drops his arms and laughs. "Man, what *was* that in there? I can't even get you to raise your hand in class when you know the right answer!"

"Yeah," Holly says, looking sideways at me. "Is this what you're like when you're bored and we've just never seen you this bored before?"

"The movie didn't bore me." I try to sound more casual than I feel. "It *offended* me."

"It's just a fantasy," Holly says.

"She didn't love him," I say. "Being in love with someone who doesn't love you back is a tragedy. A fantasy is having someone understand the real you and love you anyway."

"Yeah," Declan says. "And having someone be exactly what you want every single moment is a *perverse* fantasy... like dating your English butler."

Holly thinks about this until Declan says, "Forget it, Holly. Your life isn't a movie."

She sighs. "Sure isn't." Then she stops his reply with a quick kiss. "Okay," Holly says to me. "I didn't know you had it in you, but maybe you saved lives in there. A much-needed wake-up call."

"Maybe," I say, starting to come down from the adrenaline of my outburst, getting my head back, and feeling the first pangs of regret. "But it's not nice to go to someone else's church and make fun of them. I knew the movie would be like that. They didn't force me to come."

Declan says to Holly, "I guess it's our fault, then."

"It's nobody's fault," Holly says firmly. "Movie Roulette. Whatever starts next, no exceptions."

"Yeah," I say. "Except *we* made that rule."

"*You* made it," Declan says to Holly. "It's your fault."

"Fine," she says. "Want me to go back and apologize, or drive us to get frozen yogurt?"

"I don't feel like yogurt," I say, hoping to bail out early. Even on normal days I can only socialize for so long without recharging. Although that wasn't always true. I never needed to recharge when I was with Zumi.

"Something else, then?" Holly asks. "I'm not going home till midnight no matter what. There's no way I'm going back before curfew just to get stuck between Angie and Vicki's never-ending argument."

Declan says, "You don't know how good you've got it. I wish I had siblings to reduce my time under the microscope and my parents' questions."

"I can't remember the last time someone at home asked me a meaningful question," Holly says. "With sisters who've been fighting since before I was born, I'm ignored like dining room furniture."

56

"I could use some ignored time," Declan says. "Apparently I'm an only child on purpose. My mom says it's because they couldn't improve on perfection. My dad says I was a terrible mistake they didn't want to repeat. What about you, Mel? Why didn't your parents have any other kids?"

The question catches me off guard. I hope I don't look startled.

"I don't know," I manage to say. "It's not a conversation we've ever had."

———

I ask Holly to drop me off at work so I can check on something, which is true. They know it's a 24/7 kind of place, and not a long walk from my house, so they aren't surprised.

Standing outside the Silver Sands makes me think of Grandma Cece. I wonder if Holly invited me out tonight to make up for what Declan said yesterday about stealing cancer brownies. Grandma Cece died around the time I met them. I only mentioned it to Holly once but her superpower must be remembering stuff.

Inside the Silver Sands, most of the residents are in their rooms. I walk down the hall to Room 108. The crack under the door is glowing. I knock lightly. Ms. Li said she wasn't hard of hearing.

Her muffled voice says, "Hello?"

"It's Mel," I whisper. "Just checking on you."

Shuffling footsteps. The door unlocks and opens. Ms. Li wears a floor-length red-and-black floral housecoat.

"Sorry to bother you this late. I wanted to see how you're doing. Need anything?"

"Please come in."

A game of solitaire is laid out on her otherwise bare desk. The room is decked out with her own furniture but the open cardboard boxes scattered around are still filled with all sorts of other stuff. New residents often take a while to unpack. Dr. Jordan told me that even those who are glad to be moving in don't rush because they realize it's possibly the last time they'll ever do it.

"Not tired?" I say. "Me neither. You like solitaire?"

"I like gin rummy better."

I smile.

She doesn't, but her eyes crinkle at the corners.

After no more than ten minutes of playing, three hands at most—and she wins them all—I say something about how long we've gone without rain.

Ms. Li flaps her hands, face puckering like she'd bitten a moldy grape. "I'm too old to waste time talking about things we both know! Tell me who's who and what's what around here."

And so it goes. Hours later it's clear she didn't just want some orientation. She really has no patience for small talk. Nothing we discuss is trivial, and somehow, around two in the morning, when she finally starts nodding off and I say good night, I head for home fully recharged despite having had no time to myself. It's something I haven't felt in over a year.

EIGHT

Hamster is *Running*

Hummingbird is *Perched*

Hammerhead is *Cruising*

Hanniganimal is *Down / Mixed*

My alarm goes off at 6:15 a.m. Needing to wake up this early on weekends is the least of my problems but it's still pretty depressing. Especially after only three hours' sleep.

I dig the pills I need out of plastic bottles clustered on my nightstand. I set them down one at a time to make a big letter *M* so I won't forget any...a quetiapine...a tab of oxcarbaze-pine...topiramate...bupropion...and a Ritalin cap. I grab my water bottle and swallow pills one at a time to get myself to drink enough to dissolve them all. Finally I collapse on my bed, pull up the covers, and...*shit*. It's Saturday. I shouldn't have taken the Ritalin. Damn it.

I want to curl up in bed with the curtains closed, sleep in my dark, stuffy room, and if it doesn't stay stuffy enough, turn on the space heater till it is. I feel lethargic, hopeless, with

59

a strong urge to accept this and even indulge it. Most of my cocktail is for stabilizing my moods but the Ritalin is to fix my thinking, only now it's making trouble. Like when a little kid is exhausted and fights it, getting more irritable and cranky, until she totally melts down.

I'm the opposite. All of me votes to stay in bed, sinking away from this messy, impossible world, hiding, dozing, except for the part of my brain the Ritalin's revving up to say *oh no, that's not* going to happen: veto, *veto, VETO*! And it's right. I shouldn't spend Saturday in bed...but I did stay up most of the night....

Yet I can tell sleep isn't going to come. Staying in bed would just be to hide. And God, do I want to hide.

When I told Dr. Jordan about this feeling, he said that in the most typical example of an obsessive-compulsive disorder, you might be afraid of germs, but washing your hands can make the obsession stronger. It might feel a bit better while you're doing it, but it keeps you thinking about the germs, so you keep on scrubbing and scrubbing.

He told me the best way to escape a cycle like that isn't to try to fulfill what your mind says it wants, but to distract it with something else entirely. And it works. I've done it. I know how to break this spell. But it's still incredibly hard to do. I mean, sure, I won't fall back asleep, but what's the harm in staying in my warm bed a bit longer? It's early on a Saturday, it's chilly out, and I won't stay here all day, just another hour or so....

Except Annie's back on my mind. On my driveway. And her box is in my closet.

I throw off the comforter and sit up. It takes all my strength not to flop down again.

———

To the east is a light patch in the low gray clouds where the sun should be. The air is cold. The aluminum bench I'm sitting on is colder. Everything about the vacant high school track and surrounding bleachers looks cold this morning.

I discovered the benefit of coming here almost exactly a year ago, by accident. The meds were starting to work but I was still struggling with every single aspect of daily life. Holly and Declan were keeping me afloat, but they had other friends, and I needed to keep some distance from everyone to hide what was happening to me. I also needed lots of alone time. I spent lunches pacing the school grounds nibbling on an apple, the only food I could get myself to eat during the day through the barricade of medication side effects.

Track and field was in full swing. People were running and jumping and throwing discus and shot-putting. I was wandering in a haze and sat on the bleachers. After a few minutes I started to feel better. Only then did I realize I was sitting directly across from the long jump pit. It shocked me. This was the last place I thought would settle me, but it did, no denying it.

Nolan wanted more than anything to be on the team. He didn't care how, as long as he was *doing* something—that's how he put it—which meant field events. The coaches caught on pretty quickly that they couldn't trust him to handle gear safely—no discus, no hammer throw, definitely no pole-vaulting. The perfect event for him was the long jump: no heavy objects, no throwing anything, just run like hell for a short burst and jump.

I only know this because I was told; I was in middle school at the time. I never saw Nolan compete since he never made the team. His GPA wasn't high enough. I think they let him come to practice anyway for some reason, maybe to inspire him to bring his grades up.

I don't know why sitting here soothes me. Most of the time I don't even think about Nolan. I just watch the jumpers and get some kind of relief, though from what I don't really know. I come here before school most mornings now, sometimes finishing last-minute homework, other times just sitting here feeling a bit of peace.

I've never tried long jumping myself, but I've learned a lot from sitting here: how you're supposed to run, jump, and land. I also know the distances they clear, both the best jumpers and the worst. But I'll never know how far Nolan could jump.

This morning, sitting here in the cold, it's not calming me. Maybe because the track is empty. Maybe because my bike is parked nearby with Annie's box strapped on the back. Or maybe because of this nagging thought that being here isn't a good idea. That I'm distracting myself from one obsession by retreating into a different one.

———

I ride over to the Silver Sands midmorning. I'm not ready to face Zumi yet. Maybe spending a few hours with other people will get me out of my head. I'm still feeling off balance, but I don't need to be a genius at work. Officially I'm a gofer—here to fetch things, clean up messes, do odd jobs—though Judith says she mostly pays me for what she calls "Mel's Magic." I think this means me being everyone's granddaughter who visits almost every day.

Mr. Terrance Knight smiles when I walk into the Beach-front Lounge. I recognize the question on his face. The Han-niganimal is definitely not Up, but it looks like he needs this. The whole room feels cloudy and in need of sunshine. I put on my bright smile.

"What's it gonna be?" Mr. Terrance Knight asks me as he carefully lowers himself onto the piano bench. "Your favorite?"

"What about *your* favorite?"

"How about the room's favorite?" Mr. Terrance Knight begins to play. I smile when I recognize the song, and we come in together....

"I am dreaming, Dear, of you...day...by...day...Dreaming when the skies are blue...When...they're...gray...When the silv'ry moonlight gleams...Still I wander on, in dreams... In a land of love, it seems...Just...with...you..."

Much of the room joins in....

"Let me call you 'Sweetheart'...I'm in love...with... you...Let me hear you whisper that you love...me...too... Keep the love light glowing...in your eyes...so...true...Let me call you 'Sweetheart'...I'm in love...with...you..."

Everyone lets Mr. Terrance Knight and me sing the verses alone and they only sing the chorus. When we finish, we bow to the usual applause.

I gear up for another—I rarely get away with less than three—but Mr. Terrance Knight struggles to his feet and shuffles toward the window table where a couple other residents are playing cribbage. As he passes me, he gives me a look and nods toward the hallway. Standing there is the guy who chased me away from Ms. Li yesterday. Last night I learned he's her grandson, David. He's leaning against the wall like he's been there awhile.

All those hours getting to know Ms. Li, we only talked about him a little. She said he was very close to his uncle Miles, her son whose heart stopped beating the previous weekend. She also said David was unhappy she moved to the Silver Sands instead of his house, but he understood her not wanting to be alone most of the time with everyone away at work and school.

He pushes off and walks over. I wonder if he's going to snap at me again. It's okay if he does—working here frequently makes me a target of misdirected emotions—I know it's not personal. I just try to warm everything up, even when I'm not feeling particularly warm myself. It's my job.

"Wow," he says in a neutral tone. He's doing this thing where his face is kind of sour except his eyes are open and relaxed, just like Ms. Li's.

"Wow?" I say.

"As in, wow, you sing."

I shrug. "Only because I love hearing Mr. Terrance Knight sing, and he won't unless I join him."

"Ah," he says, as if this explains something.

He glances around, and then he leans forward, like

he's about to tell me something awkward. I feel a shot of adrenaline—is there toilet paper hanging out of my scrubs? Or worse?

He whispers, "You're a *terrible* singer."

I bark out a laugh. I hear a bit of Hurricane Joan in it.

"No, please, don't hold back! If people aren't honest with me, I'll never get any better!"

David says somberly, "Glad to help."

It's true I'm a bad singer, but I can tell he's just teasing. His straight face didn't make it easy, though. I might not have realized it had I not just spent hours with his grandmother, getting a comprehensive lesson on the Li sense of humor, which clearly they share.

"Ms. Li tells me you're a full David, not Davey or Dave anymore." I stick out my right hand. "I'm Mel Hannigan." I twist my other hand around to point at my name tag. "Yes, that's my real name. No, it's not a nickname."

"So...you really want to shake my hand?" He says. Then, in a stuffy voice, *"It's a pleasure to meet you."*

I drop my hand, embarrassed. Then I see his eyes crinkle....

"Oh, I get it." I nod wisely. "You don't like touching girls. That's okay. Didn't mean to put you on the spot there."

He smiles. Then his eyebrows drop down a notch. "My grandmother says you played cards with her way past midnight. Thank you."

"It was fun," I say. "She's a shark. Good thing we weren't playing for money. I'm afraid to play poker with her."

"Yes, definitely be afraid of that," he says. "Anyway, I wanted to say thanks...and...I'm sorry I was a jerk yesterday."

"I'm sorry about your uncle."

I touch his forearm. It's a reflex; I do it with residents all the time without thinking about it anymore. This is different but I realize it too late. I pull back as casually as I can while hoping my face isn't turning as red as it feels.

"Thanks," he says. "I have to get back. We're unpacking all her stuff."

"Okay. But...more importantly...about my singing?"

"Right, my honest opinion...A for effort. And guts."

"Don't worry; I'll keep my day job."

I watch David cross the room and disappear down the hall. I've heard people say only good friends can tease like we just did. I've never told anyone, but I don't think talking this way is a reward. It's an invitation, to skip over all that shaking hands and small talk nonsense and get on with the real stuff.

I accept.

———

Around noon I'm finally up to riding over to Zumi's, or at least I can't put it off anymore. When I get there no one answers the door. The car is gone, assuming they still have the same one. I'm partly relieved. But I can't just leave the box on her porch.

I ride over to Connor's. I feel bad about leaving him the box and the news, but it'll be better coming from him. He and Zumi have been best friends since diapers. Their moms joke about how they were thrown together so soon after being born that they imprinted on each other.

When Connor answers the door I can't tell if he's surprised to see me. Before I can say anything, the door opens wider and there's Zumi.

"What are you doing here?" she says, glancing at Connor like maybe he knows.

"I...I went to your house first." I hold out the box. "This is for you guys."

Connor reaches for it but Zumi stops him and asks, "What is it?"

"It's some of your stuff, I guess. From Annie. She dropped it off last night—"

Zumi snorts. "Annie went to your house? I doubt it."

I just stand there. I don't know how to tell her what happened.

Connor steps forward again and takes the box. He sets it on the porch and pops it open. Whatever's in there—I can't see from here—makes Zumi's face pinch.

"She gave this to *you*?" The anger is gone from her voice, replaced by bewilderment. "Why? Have you guys been talking?"

"No, she just showed up. She...she said they're moving to Paris. They left last night—"

Zumi's puzzlement disappears and she rolls her eyes. She squats by the box and pokes around. She picks up an old sweatshirt of Connor's that I recognize from the splash of green paint on it. "Come on, tell the truth for once. Where did you really get—" She stops abruptly.

"I don't know why she gave this to me," I say. "I think she just couldn't face telling you good-bye. Maybe she—"

"Get your keys," Zumi says to Connor. "We're going over there."

"Now?" he says. He looks like he's about to argue, but then he softens and reaches inside the house to the bowl by the door and grabs his car keys.

Zumi stands and walks by me. Connor closes the door and follows her.

"What about the box?" I say. "Do you want—"

"Just leave it!" Zumi calls back over her shoulder. "Just... just *leave*."

They climb into Connor's car and drive away.

I look in the box. On the top of miscellaneous knickknacks is a framed photo of the three of them in the seventh grade. Annie stands by monkey bars, her arms crossed, trying to look cool. Connor sits on a high bar, and Zumi hangs upside down by her knees between them, arms outstretched, her stomach showing. The few times I saw the inside of Annie's bedroom, this photo sat on her dresser. She said it was a present from Zumi on her twelfth birthday.

NINE

Hamster is ACTIVE

Hummingbird is HOVERING

Hammerhead is CRUISING

Hanniganimal is DOWN

HJ stands nose to nose with herself at the bathroom mirror again. I'm on the toilet lid, knees under my chin, not closely observing the process. Saturday night is prime TV binge-watching night, but I'm feeling...disconnected. Maybe I should go back to the Silver Sands. I could help Ms. Li set up her room if they're not done. When I left, David was still there with his parents working to help her get settled. It's unusual for someone his age not to cut out first chance they get—

"Mel?"

I realize it's the third time HJ has said my name. She's holding her eyeliner pencil high, ready to draw freckles on her bare spot, watching me.

"Hmm?"

"Something wrong?"

"Nope."

"You sure?" she asks. When I nod, she says, "You doing anything tonight?"

"Nope."

She looks back to the mirror, at her eyes, not her cheek.

"Fuck it." She tosses the pencil on the shelf. "Yes you are."

She turns the water on full blast, hits the soap plunger a few times, and rubs her face hard with both hands. The same way I do every afternoon for work.

"Aunt Joan?"

She buries her face in a towel. Ms. Joan Patterson, Sexy Paralegal by day, Man Hunter by night, disappears completely, and out comes Joanie, the wild red tower I remember from when I was little. Without artificial color, her face looks like a sepia photograph. I want her to look in the mirror and see how beautiful she is without paint, but she'd never believe it. She wants to be a sultry femme fatale, not the hippie tomboy she was born to be, the loud girl who refused to let me call her Aunt Joan for years because despite being in her twenties, she was still "too young" to be an aunt.

"What are you doing?" I say. "It's Saturday Night. Date Night."

"Beach Night. Put on warm clothes. It gets cold."

"Now? For how long?"

"Till it gets warm again. Dress in layers." HJ turns her head. "Pats! Beach Night!"

"Oh, Christ," Mom says in the living room, like she's talking to herself.

"Coming?"

I hear ruffling pages of whatever book or magazine she's reading. "Um...no?"

HJ turns back to me. "She's coming."

———

Hurricane Joan earns her nickname again by tossing heaps of clutter into her car: beach chairs, blankets, a big cooler, bags filled with all sorts of stuff including one with split wood from an ancient pile in the backyard. A few times Mom tries to put something back and HJ grabs it again.

Once while HJ is outside at the car, Mom says to me, "You nervous?"

"No." I'm a bit anxious, though, like I felt when Nolan would ramp up.

"You should be. Lucky for all of us, this is the *happy fun* version of not taking your meds. Let's hope it's as far as she goes."

By the time we climb into HJ's Honda, I can barely squeeze in the back with everything else—sleeping bags?!—and can't get my seat belt on. The beach is only ten minutes away, though, with no freeways. I don't fear for my life.

Instead of turning into the beach lot, HJ parks across the street. I figure this is because the parking lot closes at ten p.m. It takes us four trips across the street to the particular spot on the sand where HJ insists we camp. The sun is about to drop into the ocean when we finally start setting up.

On the upside, the blankets, chairs, and sleeping bags, still rolled up, form a picturesque camp, including a fire pit made from nearby rocks piled around a pit HJ digs in the sand. It's elaborate and looks planned, like we're campers from out of town who do this a lot.

On the downside, the cooler and bags are full of random kitchen stuff: cans of beans and fruit cocktail but no can opener, glass jars of mayonnaise and pickles, a carton of orange juice, like she mindlessly swept whole shelves out of the fridge. I see Mom wince when she comes across things like a week's worth of deli ham—it'll definitely go bad out here—and she smiles wistfully to me.

Mom and I pile up unreasonable amounts of meat and cheese to make sandwiches while HJ struggles to build a fire. After minutes of frustration, she rips the spout off the lighter fluid and gleefully dumps out the entire contents. Mom and I cower on the far side of the blanket as HJ drops a match and crows at the eruption.

All at once, commotion turns to calm. We sit in beach chairs, the fire between us and the sea, the sun almost below the horizon, wiggling our toes in the warm sand at the edge of the blanket, eating around the edges of sandwiches too tall to fit in our mouths.

"Know what I think at times like this?" HJ says to me. "How much your dad would love being out here with us."

Mom and I laugh and spew bits of bread and meat to sizzle in the fire. HJ rocks back in her chair and cackles.

"Hey!" she says. "Sun's almost down! Look for the green flash!"

Some guy she knew—I never call them boyfriends—told her sometimes you can see a flash of green at the horizon just after sunset. Probably a line about the color of her eyes. She's been looking for it ever since. I guess it's a real thing if you Google it, but HJ wants to see it in person and never has. Including tonight.

"Someday..." She sips her beer. "Someday..."

"Good evening, ladies," a man says. A cop in uniform steps over from the parking lot.

HJ smiles big. "Good evening, Officer."

"Are you not aware fires aren't allowed on the beach outside the fire rings?"

"Sorry. We made it here for the best view. We'll let it die out."

"That's fine. But the beach closes at ten." He points at the sleeping bags. "No staying overnight."

"It's still March," HJ says. "It gets cold enough for sleeping bags way before ten. Who tries to stay out here all night?"

"It's *usually* people who have nowhere else to stay. I'm going to drive by later to make sure you've cleared out."

"Of course. About when, do you think?"

I stare at her. Does she think she's subtle?

"At the end of my shift, around midnight."

HJ smiles. "You won't see us."

"All right, you ladies have a good night." He turns to leave but then stops. "Seriously, Joan, make sure the fire's out by ten. And no lights or my new shift commander will see you."

"Jesus, Tom, I'm not a rookie. We're south of the fire rings for a reason. I've been doing this since you were in high school."

73

"And *you* were in *junior* high." He adjusts his belt. "It's Sunday Shots tomorrow night at the Rockin' Pony. You coming?"

"Does the Pope shit in the woods?"

He grins. "See you there."

As he leaves, Mom rolls her eyes. HJ smiles like she ate a canary.

"You've done this for years?" I say. "How come I never knew?"

"Haven't for a while. Besides, you weren't old enough."

"I am now? If the magic number's seventeen, that's weeks away. And he said you were doing it in middle school. You were thirteen?"

"Age has nothing to do with numbers, Mel."

———

Mom doesn't like the cold, or being away from home, or worrying about getting in trouble with the police, but she likes being awake at night even less. She's in her sleeping bag, snoring lightly, by eleven.

HJ and I are experts at staying awake but we're nonetheless bundled up in sleeping bags against the cold. With no lights or moon, no one could possibly see us out here. Dad would have a fit. This is way worse than parking bikes in the house.

"I worry about you, Mel."

Uh-oh.

"Is that why we're on the beach, risking arrest, at…" I check my phone. "One fifteen?"

"*Pffft*. Tom wouldn't arrest me. He knows he can always ask me for a dance and get a boost from a girl saying yes. Just not slow dances. You can't tell I have four inches on him if he doesn't pull me close. Then we look like a kid dancing with his mom." She laughs. "Nobody wants that image in the room. Perfect recipe for going home alone."

We lie quietly for a moment.

"Didn't work," she says.

"What?"

"Trying to change the subject."

I'd forgotten how this outing started, with HJ abruptly washing off her game face like she had a new mission. Whatever it is, it's starting. The most I can do is deflect.

"I worry about you," she says again.

"Not as much as I worry about you."

"I'm not the one doped up all the time! You put more drugs in your system than Grandma did when she was fighting cancer!"

Okay, it's *that* conversation. I try to look on the bright side, that she can bring up Grandma Cece easily now. It used to be a big deal. When Grandma died, we lost HJ for a couple months.

"They suck all the life out of you, like there's a wet blanket on you all the time."

Usually I can get out of these talks all kinds of ways, but not trapped in a sleeping bag on a dark beach in the middle of the night.

I sigh. "I don't like who I am without the meds—" Oops,

that was a mistake. I should have stuck with one of my vague responses.

"But that's who you are!" HJ rolls on her side to face me directly. "Those pills turn you into someone who wants to hang out with old people or stay at home all the time. You're almost seventeen! I don't think I've ever seen you try a beer! Have you?"

"Yeah. They're gross."

She laughs. "You get used to it."

"I don't want to get used to it." Or lots of other things I've seen Aunt Joan get used to.

"I'm not telling you to drink. I just hate seeing you miss out on your teenage years because of those pills."

We've had this conversation countless times, when Mom's not around to stop her. Except I know the drugs are a scapegoat. Like how Dad thinks I'm unambitious and unmotivated and blames it on being surrounded by underachievers. Aunt Joan thinks I'm antisocial because of the meds. They're both wrong. I'm naturally an antisocial underachiever.

HJ tried meds and didn't like them. Her mood swings aren't nearly as fast or extreme as mine, and she doesn't get mixed states like I do. On the severity scale, HJ's about a six, and the happy sex-crazed kind of bipolar disorder, not the angry delusional kind. With my medication cocktail, I'm a four and mostly on the depressed side. Without my meds, I'm seven or eight and prone to manic episodes. And Nolan, he—whoa! Stop right there....

Point is, some remember the ups and downs, and others

forget. I'm lucky I remember. The forgetters, like HJ, they get right and then believe they don't need meds anymore, completely forgetting how they came unhinged every other time they stopped. Or they miss the joys of being supercharged and forget the crushing lows. Or how the supercharging sometimes overloads and makes them do things they regret: go broke, land in jail, hurt people—themselves, or much worse.

"You're not sick, Mel. None of us are."

She's not going to let it go. Maybe it's time to try this again.

"Fine, but when I come out of an episode, all I can think is, who *was* that person? Why did she lie in bed all weekend thinking everything was too pointless to bother getting up? And then why'd she jump out of bed and stay up all night believing she could learn Portuguese by morning, thinking it's just Spanish with a few different words? Even if it was true—and it's not—I hardly know any Spanish! The meds keep me from turning into those other people."

"Those people *are* you. They're just moods."

"Trying to learn Portuguese overnight isn't a *mood*. It's someone else jumping into my head and grabbing the controls. I still have moods on my meds; I just don't get *possessed*, thinking and feeling and *doing* all this random shit."

She doesn't answer. I can't see her face in the dark.

I say, "Maybe you just don't think about things like I do."

"I don't think about things? All I want is a good time?"

"That's not what I meant—"

"I know moods can feel like different people," HJ says. "But you've picked one and decided it's the only real you. How

77

77

do you know it's the right one? I think you just picked the safest choice."

"It's who I am when I'm level."

"It's not the only real you! The drugs chop off the highs and lows so all you're left with is the one who doesn't have highs or lows! That's why you don't go out, take chances, put yourself out there, be a teenager."

"I'm surrounded by teenagers at school," I say. "Only a few of them are party monsters or serial daters or sluts—" *Fuck!*

"Is that what you think I am?"

"No! I'm saying those are stereotypes, not what all teenagers actually do. A lot of people I know don't party or have boyfriends or girlfriends or even go out much."

HJ is quiet.

Goddamn it, this is why I can't talk about this. I really need to keep my mouth shut. I don't even know what the word *slut* means here. It's a judgment and I don't judge her. I don't care if she sleeps with every guy in town if it makes her happy. I just know it doesn't.

"I'm saying I'm different, that's all. It's got nothing to do with meds. Nobody else thinks it's wrong that I work at a retirement home and don't go to parties or out on dates every weekend or have a boyfriend. Nobody but you."

After a moment, HJ says, "I don't think you're wrong, Mel. I just think you're missing out. It's a shame. Soon you won't be a teenager anymore, and you'll never be one again."

We say no more about it. Or anything else.

TEN

Hamster is *ACTIVE*

Hummingbird is *FLYING*

Hammerhead is *CRUISING*

Hanniganimal is *UP!*

We haul our sandy gear home at sunrise ahead of the rising tide. I feel a lot better this morning after sleeping some. Unnaturally upbeat, actually, given the circumstances. It happens. I'm embracing it. HJ would approve.

I remember to skip the Ritalin part of my medication *M*, and now I'm famished. That problem's easily solved. The Silver Sands has a great breakfast buffet.

I pile my plate with scrambled eggs, bacon, home fries, wheat toast, and apple slices, and I grab a glass of orange juice. Most of the residents have eaten and drifted out. Dr. Jordan is doing a crossword puzzle next to an empty plate. Ms. Li sits alone, halfway through an omelet and nursing a cup of tea.

I cross over to her table. "Mind if I join you?"

"Going farming today?" she asks.

"If farming means lying on a couch reading a book."

I'm not on the clock till after I eat so I haven't changed into scrubs; I'm wearing Mom's baggy overalls. I looked in the dryer for something clean to put on this morning and this was my choice. Mom made some crack about it being unfair, since she couldn't fit into my jeans from the same load. I expressed no sympathy. I claimed it as my reward for emptying the dryer.

Ms. Li waves me into a chair.

I say, "I see you already figured out the best thing here is the veggie omelet."

"Why didn't you get one?"

"Too much green and not enough bacon for this early. I like them for dinner."

David says, "Gone two minutes and you give away my chair."

I jump, startled. Ms. Li never glanced up to give me a clue.

"Oh, sorry!" I start to stand. "I didn't—"

"It's fine; don't move your breakfast." He sits in another chair. "You're here early."

"I work here. I eat here. Sometimes both."

"I need to find a job that pays me to eat."

"Don't be jealous—go grab a plate," I say. "There's bacon left."

"I'm fine."

"No, really, tell them Mel said it's okay. It's nice and crispy today."

"I don't eat bacon."

"Huh?" I peer at him.

He leans forward and enunciates carefully. "I . . . don't . . . eat . . . bacon."

I look to Ms. Li. "What'd he say? Was it Chinese?"

She scoffs. "He couldn't order off the menu in a Chinese restaurant." She scoops up a heaping forkful of eggs. "He's a *vegetarian*."

David leans back. "Says the woman eating a veggie omelet."

She shrugs.

"Pro-health?" I ask. "Pro-environment? Anti-cruelty?"

He doesn't answer, but he doesn't look away.

I sip my orange juice and also don't look away.

"I'm Jewish."

I choke. Now I have to wipe orange juice off my chin.

Ms. Li laughs loudly and slides over her spare napkins.

"Not really," David says. "It's all those other things." Then he cocks his head and asks, mock-innocent, "But what's so funny about me being Jewish?"

Damn, he's good at this. I have to step up my game....

"You *could* be," I say, leaning in. "But I assumed you were Catholic."

"Uh..." He draws back. "Why?"

"She said you go to Blessed Heart. Though I guess it could be because it's the best private school around."

"Oh, right." He smiles, as if to say I won that round.

I say, "Does the fact that I love bacon mean we can't be friends?"

"It only means you can't be friends with pigs. Certain pigs, anyway. And don't worry...." He leans forward again. "You liking different things is fine. It's no fun talking to a mirror."

I laugh, but he doesn't. Wait... did he really mean that last part?

Ms. Li laughs and blurts something in Chinese.

David grins big—the first I've seen from him. Nope, not serious. His grandmother told me he's hardly ever serious but his poker face is amazing. He laughs and bows his head, and this instantly triggers my bright smile. That almost never happens on its own.

"What?" I say. "I thought you didn't speak Chinese?"

"I understand some Mandarin. Mostly things she says to me a lot. She said I'm full of shit."

I laugh. "Are you?"

"Completely," he says. "But I promise you, it's good honest shit."

It's funny, but it also feels true. I expect him to look away, like how people do when they admit things. He doesn't. In fact, the whole time we've been talking, except when he briefly bowed his head, David's dark brown eyes haven't looked away from mine. Not even a flicker.

———

A couple of hours later I'm playing cribbage in the Beachfront Lounge. I can hold my own, meaning I don't embarrass myself, but Mr. Terrance Knight usually wins. At all games, not just cribbage.

I get a phone call. The buzzing stops the moment I see it's from Zumi.

"Something wrong?" Mr. Terrance Knight asks.

"No," I say. "I…"

No voice mail pops up but it's only been a few seconds. It didn't ring enough times to go to voice mail anyway. She must have hung up.

"It's fine," I say.

It's not fine. I want to call her back. But if she hung up, then maybe she doesn't want to talk after all. Or the call might have dropped—that happens sometimes here on the coast—

Mr. Terrance Knight says, "This can wait if you want to call 'em back."

I do, though not if she changed her mind. But I also don't want her thinking I'm ignoring that she called.

I text her:

Want to talk?

I set the phone down and resume the game.

We finish ten minutes later with no more signs of life from my phone. I excuse myself and head for the Sun Room.

Maybe she didn't see my text. I try again:

Zumi?

No reply. I sit on the sofa facing the south window and text Connor:

You with Zumi?

Connor texts back:

Not going well got to go

I text him:

Should I come?

83

I'm sure Judith wouldn't mind me leaving now since I came to work early. I'm not really on that strict a schedule anyway.

No answer. Maybe I should just go. That's what Zumi would do.

———

July after freshman year, Annie's in Connecticut with her family for a week. When we're with her, we're always doing stuff like crawling the mall or walking the beach or riding our bikes somewhere. It's like she always wants to be seeing other people, or be seen by them, even if we're not actually with them. While she's away, we hang out all day at Connor's. His house has the best food and the fewest number of other people; just his mom, and she hits the perfect mix of giving us snacks and leaving us alone.

Often we're all three together on the living room sofa, talking or watching TV, but today we're in Connor's room. He sits at his desk, Web surfing, trying to ignore us while Zumi and I sprawl on the bed and make fun of his shelves: how his books and DVDs are mixed together but they're all in alphabetical order, and how he has every Disney movie ever made, including stuff like The Little Mermaid. *He says we're just jealous that he has them all, and he's right.*

"What are you even doing over there?" Zumi asks him.

"Checking for new doppelgängers."

Zumi rolls her eyes. She sees me looking confused and says, "He's Googling his name again."

"Ha," I say. "The Internet doesn't know who you are, Connor."

"Doppelgängers," he says again. "I once found a Connor

Lewis on a hockey team in Canada—I don't remember which one—and he looked a lot like me, just older, and with a nose that'd been broken a bunch of times. Kind of scary."

"There's a ton of me's out there," Zumi says. "And...surprise!" She rolls on her back and throws out her arms. "They're all Japanese!"

I laugh.

Zumi rolls back on her stomach. "What about Mel?"

"Let's see..." Connor says, typing.

"I know," Zumi says. "There's probably a mechanic out there named Mel Hannigan—maybe he owns his own shop." She makes air quotes. "Hannigan's Car Repair."

I shove her and she almost falls off the bed. "Hey!" she says and shoves me back.

"This is weird," Connor says. "Here's a kid named Nolan Hannigan where you used to live. Did you know him?"

I freeze. Zumi jumps off the bed and stands behind Connor to look at the screen.

"This says he died there...a couple years ago...."

Zumi lowers her chin to rest on Connor's shoulder, reading. "God...this is horrible...."

I stand and walk over. I can't focus on the screen.

"This was before you moved," Zumi says. "How could you not have heard about this?"

All I can do is shake my head. I can't speak. I'm getting dizzy....

Connor says something else. Zumi answers. Their words are out of reach. I can't see very well. My jaw clenches so hard I can feel my teeth spreading.

I pull my phone out of my pocket and pretend to answer it. "What? Okay. Be right there." I put it away. "My mom. Gotta... do something...."

Zumi follows me down the hall. "Mel? Wait!"

I open the front door.

"Did your mom really call? I didn't hear your phone." She grabs my arm—I pull away.

Next I'm facedown on my bed with hardly any memory of climbing on my bike or pedaling home. The house is empty with everyone else at work. I think my bike fell over in the entryway and I left it—I'm not sure. I don't remember when I started crying.

"Mel?"

I don't know how I can be hearing Zumi now, alone in my room, over the roaring in my ears. I also can't see anything with my eyes squeezed shut.

"I'm going to pop the screen out," she says.

"Wait," Connor says. "Maybe she—"

"Can't you hear her?!"

"Yeah, but she might want—"

"Boost me up."

A stack of books falls over. My desk lamp clatters.

"Mel," Connor's voice says from the window. "Do you want us to go?"

I push my face into the pillow.

The bed sinks from added weight.

"You can talk to us," Zumi says. She puts a gentle hand on my back. "Do you want to?"

I shake my head.

86

"Not now? Or...not ever?"

I nod at that, hard enough to hurt, and wrap my arms around my head.

My desk lamp rattles again. I hear books being stacked.

Zumi pulls on me, carefully. When I don't cooperate, she lies down beside me, on her side, and rubs my back.

"Connor," she whispers. "Sandwich."

"You think maybe—"

"Stop thinking!"

The bed shifts again, on the other side. I feel Connor lie down on his back next to me.

"If you want to be alone," Zumi whispers, "just say so."

I don't say so.

"And you're still an only child until you tell us you're not. We...we won't even tell Annie. Right, Connor?"

I sob. I hope they understand it's the closest I can come to saying thank you.

———

Zumi and Connor stayed with me for hours that day. When I finally sat up, Zumi said, "You have all the *Toy Story* movies, right? Let's watch the second one. The one where Woody can't decide whether to go away to Japan. That's the most fun because I can't decide which way to root for."

After that, it was like it never happened. I saw no glimmer, no hint, not even a meaningful look when similar subjects came up. I've never told them how much their silence, and them climbing through my window, was exactly what I needed.

Zumi didn't wait for me to ask her to come over. She never asked; she just did things. I text Connor again:

> I'm coming.

Except they could be anywhere.

> Where are you guys?
> Zumi's house?

I head up the hall to retrieve my stuff and find Judith. Before I get far, my phone buzzes.

> **She says she wants to be alone.**

ELEVEN

Hamster is *Running*

Hummingbird is *Flying*

Hammerhead is *Cruising*

Hanniganimal is *Down / Mixed*

Monday morning, between second and third period, Declan and I walk down the hall without talking. This isn't unusual. He says I get lost in my head and he just waits for me to find my way out again. He thinks it's cool I can do that without having to smoke. That's not what's going on now, though— I'm actually feeling more jumpy than lost.

"You okay?" he asks. I guess it shows.

"Just tired."

That's as much as I'm willing to say. It's true I didn't sleep last night. Mom figured it out and tried to keep me home, but I'd miss half the school year if insomnia were a reason to skip class.

I have Chemistry with Zumi, which is where Declan and I are heading now. I hope she's here today. I want to see that she's okay, even if only from a distance.

Declan says, "You hear about Annie Bridger?"

"What did *you* hear?"

"You know Holly and I have English Lit with her, or we did. Mr. Templeton said she moved to Paris. I guess her dad's been teaching at the Sorbonne this past year. Anyway, a week ago she took the proficiency exam to graduate early. She left on Friday."

"I heard." At least the last part.

"You must be glad you won't have to see her around anymore. But if you knew she was leaving, why didn't you say anything?"

"Nobody knew."

"Zumi and Connor must have."

"They didn't find out till after she'd left."

"No way. Even Annie... well, I don't know what I was going to say. Annie sure was a..."

"Go ahead," I say. "I saw the light, remember? Bash away."

"Still, what an unbelievably shitty thing to do. They've been best friends for years."

Zumi's at her lab table by the windows. She faces straight ahead, her backpack in front of her. All I can see from this angle is her wall of hair.

The bell rings. Mr. Gottfried turns from writing the day's agenda on the whiteboard and sees Zumi's backpack still on the table.

"Ms. Shimura?"

She doesn't react.

"Izumi," he says softly. "Please stow your backpack."

He rarely uses anyone's first name and he usually barks when ignored. Maybe Zumi was a topic in the staff room in addition to Annie's early graduation. Maybe all the teachers knew for weeks and Annie asked them to keep it confidential.

Zumi sweeps her arm just enough to slide her backpack off the table. It crashes to the floor. She loops her foot around the strap and drags it out of the aisle.

"Thank you."

Zumi doesn't move a muscle the whole period. When we run tests with pH strips at our desks, her lab partner, Benji, does it all. She doesn't even watch.

———

Zumi's next class is adjacent to mine. I usually walk slowly to make sure I don't catch up. Not today. I have to talk to her. Except she darts out quicker than I expect after her being still all period. I pack up quickly, say good-bye to Declan, and trot out into the hall. She's maybe twenty feet ahead.

"Hey, Z!" someone calls. My hair stands on end. Zumi hates that nickname.

"I heard you're a free agent now." It's Tina Fernandez, her voice like a knife twisting.

Zumi passes her without turning her head. Gloria opens her locker a few feet away. Elena leans against the wall but doesn't look natural doing it, playing a part she's not well suited for. I don't see Sofia, but come to think of it, I stopped seeing her with Team Fernandez months ago.

"That can't feel good," Tina says. "Who's gonna hold your leash now?"

Zumi stops. I hurry forward.

"What you think, Elena?" Tina says. "Know anyone who'd want Annie's leftovers?"

Zumi turns but I manage to get between them before she's fully around. Zumi leans back when she sees me.

"Don't, Zumi." I touch her forearm—

She recoils, wincing, and then whirls away around the corner.

Tina stands beside me. "Didn't need your help, *tontita*."

"Yes you did," I say. "But I wasn't helping you."

I round the corner and almost bump into Zumi. She's standing still, tense, facing me. Her mouth and eyes are taut like she has stomach pains.

"Zumi…" What do I say? *I'm sorry Annie abandoned you? I'm sorry I did it first?*

Finally I say, "You called me yesterday."

She doesn't reply.

I lean toward her. "Please say something."

"I called to ask why." Her voice is low and hoarse. "Why you. Then I changed my mind. I didn't want to wonder if whatever you said was a lie."

It's the perfect thing to say to render me speechless. But I have to say something.

"We hadn't talked in over a year, I swear. She just showed up."

"Connor said she gave it to you because she's a coward. What do *you* think?"

"You know what I thought of her." That's what my last argument with Zumi was about.

After a moment, she says, "Doesn't matter now."

She turns and walks away.

"Zumi, I—"

"I'm late for class."

———

I wander around most of lunch looking for Zumi and Connor. With five minutes left, I see Connor alone on the brick wall. I walk up to him and wait. Connor will talk plenty if you give him room and some indication that you'll listen and care, that his words won't be wasted on you.

He finally points to the apple in my hand. "That your whole lunch?"

"Yeah. Keeps the doctor away. Where's Zumi?"

He doesn't answer.

I take a bite of apple.

"She's already gone to Calc," he says.

I lean against the wall. "You guys had no idea at all?"

"We knew her dad was there teaching. We thought he was coming back this summer."

"Maybe that was the plan. Maybe they recently decided to move there instead."

"They didn't decide it on Friday. Annie must have been sitting on this awhile."

"What happened when you drove to her house?"

"You know how nice it was. I guess they sold it without needing to put up a sign. Zumi looked in the windows long enough to see the rooms were empty. Then she went back to the car."

"Did she cry?"

He glances at me, surprised, and then looks away again. "Zumi never cries."

"I know, but it's not like her to do *nothing*. Why isn't she pissed off? Throwing things and pounding on doors and walls and...I've just never seen her...shut down."

"You've never seen her humiliated."

"Nothing embarrasses Zumi," I say.

"Humiliated. It's different."

I climb up and sit on the wall beside him. He holds out his bag of corn chips. I shake my head.

"She'll break through it," he says. "Then she'll get pissed off and it'll all come out in flames. It always does."

The bell rings. There's more I want to talk about. No time now.

"I'm sorry," I say.

He turns his head like he's going to look at me, but he doesn't quite make it. He starts packing his lunch trash.

I stand.

"Mel?"

He takes the apple core from my hand and stuffs it into his bag.

"Thanks, Connor."

———

After school, Holly and I reach the sidewalk and Declan still hasn't joined us. Holly sits on the curb. None of her other friends are around so I join her. Today she didn't tie her hair back; it's been flopping all around, having fun. I shove my hands deep in my pockets.

Connor and Zumi drive by. It doesn't look like they're talking.

"What's up with them?" Holly asks.

"What do you mean?"

"Declan said you stared at Izumi all through Chem today."

Holly always uses her full name, believing that only her friends or ex-friends call her Zumi.

"What exactly happened between you?" Holly asks. "You know, last year?"

It's a simple question. An obvious one, too, but she's never asked before.

"Why ask now?" My tone is sharper than I intended.

She tips her head and smiles. "You were too upset last year."

"You know what Annie was like. Everybody did."

"Only from the outside. Seemed like she wanted to be queen but couldn't attract subjects. I thought Izumi and Connor stayed friends with her because none of them could do any better. Kinda sad, really."

"I guess it took me longer than most to figure her out," I say. "Pretty much all of freshman year. I tried to let it slide, but...one day I couldn't take any more and called her on her bullshit. She tried to...I don't know, pull rank, I guess. When I didn't take it back and fall in line, we were done."

"Whatever her deal was, it must have worked fine for Izumi and Connor. They didn't waste any time writing you off."

I shake my head. "Zumi hounded me for weeks. I just...
I couldn't..."

The truth is, I was the one who stopped talking. It really
hurt and confused her, I know, but I was in the middle of my
bipolar onset, fighting for my crumbling sanity and to keep the
whole battle a secret. I also wanted to protect her from what
happened with Annie. My phone still holds the history of texts
from Zumi that I never answered. I don't read them anymore,
but I can't avoid seeing the dent she made on our front door
trying to find me. Aunt Joan kept telling her I wasn't home. It
was true in a way.

"It was my fault," I say. "And I'm pretty sure Annie told
stories about me."

"They still believed her instead of you."

"Why wouldn't they? They were friends long before I got
here. And I didn't tell them Annie was lying."

It was clear from Zumi's dwindling messages that Annie
was telling her I was the one who'd been lying to her, that I
didn't care about her, that I never had, and me not answering
was slowly convincing her. Months later, the first time we saw
each other again at school, I ducked away. It probably seemed
like confirmation of every lie Annie told.

"Anyway," I say, "this all happened when I got sick and
went months without talking to anyone."

Holly's eyebrows go up. "Anyone?"

"Except you." I rest my head on her shoulder. "You know,
when you and Declan brought me all my homework and saved
me from flunking my classes and everything. I owe you big."

96

"Yes, you do. Most of my friendships are based on debt." Holly presses her temple against my head. "You know. Rescues."

"I'm trying to pay you back in installments," I say. "To make it last as long as possible."

She laughs.

I leave my head on Holly's shoulder and she lets me.

When I was missing so much school, Holly got assigned to bring me schoolwork, but she did so much more. She became my friend and kind of saved me from drowning entirely. I'm very grateful.

Part of me wishes I could tell Holly the truth. Mom and I covered up my absences saying I had mono and then bronchitis with a series of relapses. I wasn't really sick, at least not in the way where you eventually get better or die. I just found out my brain was poorly designed. It won't kill me, but I can't get right again since I was never right in the first place. I was born with faulty parts. My brain just didn't turn them on till I became a teenager, right around the time I blew up with Annie.

But I can't let anyone know what really happened, or what's wrong with me. I can't bear the thought of how they'd look at me, and treat me, if they knew how many pills I take every morning just to act more or less like everybody else.

97

TWELVE

Hamster is STUMBLING

Hummingbird is PERCHED

Hammerhead is CRUISING

Hanniganimal is DOWN

In Chemistry on Tuesday, Zumi doesn't move for the whole fifty-four minutes. At the end, when it's time to collect homework, she doesn't touch her backpack. Mr. Gottfried asks her about it and she ignores him. He tells her to stay after the bell rings. I wait outside but they take a long time and I finally leave for my next class.

At lunch I find Connor on the brick wall again. This time Zumi's with him, sitting a few feet away. They're staring off in different directions. I want to walk over, but no. I don't think that would make her feel good. I just try to take it as a positive sign that at least she's back to spending more time with Connor.

When I get to the Silver Sands after school, Dr. Jordan is talking to Judith at the reception desk. He stops when he notices me. I don't know what he sees but he comes over.

"You want to talk about it?"

"I talk to you too much. You're not my doctor."

"I'm glad. If I were, I couldn't do this."

He pulls me in for a tight hug, his arms completely around me. I'm chilled from the ride over—too much coasting through cold air on a cloudy day without enough pedaling—and he's warm from being inside. I hold on, wondering if I'll melt if I stay this way long enough.

"I'm your friend. I'll listen if you want to talk."

"Maybe later. Just one of those days."

After giving Ms. Arguello her orange juice, I take a deep breath and then breeze through the Beachfront Lounge, waving and smiling at everyone, pretending not to see Mr. Terrance Knight's hopeful expression. I'll give him a song today, just not yet.

After an hour of bustling I can't think of anything else to tidy up. I help Ms. Arguello ball up skeins of yarn and listen to her talk about her grandson's new job. When I run out of ways to put off singing with Mr. Terrance Knight, I step outside to charge up first. I sit on the steps, out of sight of reception, and massage my cheeks. So much smiling...

"Hey."

I look up, startled. David's standing over me.

"You okay?" he asks.

"Um, yeah. Just felt like, you know..."

"Like sitting out in the cold, looking at the gray sky?"

"Yep. I didn't know you were here."

"We were back in her room. Do you want to be alone?"

"No, it's fine."

"If you really came out to be by yourself, you don't have to pretend you didn't."

I'm squinting up at him—it's overcast but still bright out.

"Did you?" he asks.

I blink. "Did I what?"

"Come out here to get away from everyone?"

"Maybe just certain people."

David sits on the step below me. "Mr. Knight told me you were hiding from him."

I tense up.

"I said it probably wasn't him specifically, but he said no, he's been on God's green earth for eighty-three years and knows a thing or two about people—"

"I have to go—"

"Wait, that's not all." David climbs up to the step next to me. "He also said he just knows it means you're sad. He said, *'I encourage her to sing to lift her spirits. Where the voice goes, the heart follows.'*"

David tries to say it in Mr. Terrance Knight's buttery voice.

I smile. "What else did he say?"

"Just that he wishes you didn't think you needed to hide when you're feeling low."

"Hmph. It's my job to bring everyone up, not down."

"Is that the only reason you're here? Because it's your job?"

"No."

"I get the impression in there that if you smiled less, nobody would wish you'd stop coming around."

"You're awfully new here to know so much."

"Getting to know people quickly is a perk of avoiding small talk." He pauses. "So is this random sadness, or is something bothering you?"

I'm not used to being asked that by people I barely know. It feels like the sun coming out.

"Maybe a bit of both."

"Is it personal, or . . . ?"

"It's . . . Some friends of mine are having a hard time."

He leans back against the steps. "Bake them cookies."

I smirk. "I don't think that'll help."

"Oatmeal raisin."

"Yuck! Raisins in cookies are broken promises. Worse, it's betrayal."

"They'll appreciate the thought. And if they don't like how they taste, I'll eat them."

"Okay, so you *don't* eat bacon, you *do* eat gross cookies, and you give me advice to help my friends that really helps you."

"I thought everybody could win. They'd be happy you baked them something, you'd feel good about making them happy, and I'd get cookies."

"Nice try."

We're staring at each other. I like it. It's casual, and comfortable. But it's also true I'm not used to anyone staring back this long without talking. I wonder if he's aware of it, too.

A whole minute goes by. A breeze picks up. I loll my head onto my shoulder and he smiles a little. I finally say, "Okay, this can't last forever. One of us is going to have to look away first. We're not going to grow old out here together."

"I didn't know it was a contest." David looks up at the bright spot where the sun is hiding. "You win."

I roll my eyes. "You giving up doesn't make me a winner. And no, it wasn't a contest."

He looks back at me. "There's no way I'm going to cheer you up, is there?"

I quickly stand, pushing my hand down on his shoulder to help me up.

"I'm going back inside," I say. "You might want to stay out here a few minutes."

"I think they all know we're out here together."

"It's not that. I feel like singing."

———

Later, I'm with Dr. Jordan in the Sun Room, just the two of us. It's dusk, so it's even gloomier outside, but less so in my head now. He said, "Let's be ironic and play Double Solitaire," and we've been dueling for an hour.

"What do you think of David?" he asks.

I glance at him. "Very subtle."

"I know what he thinks of you."

"Because he came outside with me today?"

"Did he? I didn't know. Tell me all the deets."

I laugh. "No one says *deets* anymore. Besides, I thought you didn't like gossip."

"I don't like *admitting* I like it. Anyway, it isn't gossip if it's about you. I do admit to a certain fondness for you."

"Yeah, yeah, I know. I'm like the great-great-great-great-granddaughter you never had."

"I thank the Maker every night that it's an informal relationship."

The game enters its acceleration phase. He wins, only because I dropped my queen of hearts on the diamond stack and had to take it back and got flustered. I scoop up the cards to separate the reds from the blues.

"So, what does David think of me?"

Dr. Jordan smiles. I smile back.

"Do you care?" he asks.

"You said you knew so I'm curious. Have you even talked to him?"

"Some. But I'm a trained psychiatrist. I watch. I listen. I judge."

"And?"

"And what?"

"And this is why we don't have these kinds of conversations." I hold up the red deck of cards. "Tell me or *I'll* use your blue deck and you get these disease carriers." We needed another deck for Double Solitaire so I grabbed the red cards from the games cabinet. Dr. Jordan thinks money is the dirtiest thing around but that community playing cards are a strong second place.

"When you're not looking at him," he says, "he's looking at you."

"So? There's no one else our age here. In a room full of a hundred people and two dogs, the dogs will go sniff each other." I hand Dr. Jordan his blue deck. "Plus I know I'm...an odd thing to look at."

"How so?"

"You know. Freckles, but not the red hair or the green eyes. I'm kind of a mutt."

"Brown hair, blue eyes, and freckles doesn't make you a mutt. It's exotic."

I snort.

"It seems to work for that what's-her-name on those Hollywood news shows in the TV room. The girl who's usually in some kind of trouble."

"Maybe I'm destined for incarceration, too."

"He also makes unlikely excuses to come into whatever room you're in."

"You ready?" My solitaire staircase is done. His is only halfway there.

"I've told you about the fluoroquinolone-caused neuropathy in my hands, right?"

"About a thousand times, though I'm not sure those are the same words. You might be making up new gibberish every time. It's just an excuse for when you lose and to make me feel worse when you win."

David enters with Ms. Li on his arm. He says to her, "It's cold in here without the sun."

Dr. Jordan looks at me over his glasses.

"It isn't cold," Ms. Li says. "Is it, Mel?"

"Oh, it's definitely cold in here, but—"

"See?" David says.

"*But...*" I say, "that's why we're here. You don't want to

be comfortable *all* the time. People who do move to Florida. Don't you want to spice things up with something different sometimes?" I make meaningful eye contact with Dr. Jordan. "Maybe even something...*exotic*?"

I admire Dr. Jordan's poker face. We could take Dr. Oswald to the cleaners.

"What about you, Mr. Jordan?" David asks. "You think it's cold in here?"

"It just got chillier, you calling me that. Please, call me Piers. As for the debate, I abstain. You Californians don't know the meaning of the word *cold*."

"I know what'll warm you up," I say to David. "A shot of gin rummy."

Before he can answer, Ms. Li lets go of him and sits at our table. That leaves only the opposite chair.

"It's okay," I say. "I'll give you room. I remember you don't like touching girls."

"I guess I'm outnumbered." David's hand brushes my shoulder, as if he couldn't avoid it to get around me.

He sits. "Should we make it interesting?"

"Definitely *not*," I say. "Not for money, not for articles of clothing, not..." I falter, my face heating up. Sometimes I wish I knew what I was going to say in time to decide not to. "I'm too broke to play with this many sharks. Let's keep it just between friends for now."

David and Ms. Li exchange a glance. She nods.

He looks back to me.

"As you wish."

THIRTEEN

Hamster is *ACTIVE*

Hummingbird is *HOVERING*

Hammerhead is *CRUISING*

Hanniganimal is *LEVEL*

On Wednesday Zumi didn't show up to Chemistry. I couldn't find Connor at lunch but I saw him slip into one of his classes so I know he was at school.

Today Zumi no-shows again. I don't see Connor all day and end up spending lunch period at the track by the long jump pit.

The moment school lets out I text Connor:

Where are you?

I head for my locker to switch books. Halfway there, my phone buzzes with his answer.

Home.

Sick?

No. Study period. I leave an hour early when I don't drive Zumi home.

> You alone?

Yes.

I think for a moment, then:

> Can I come over?

Why?

> To see how you're doing.

**Zumi's still not talking
much. I don't know
anything.**

> I want to see how YOU are
> doing. I'm not coming to
> ask you anything.

I get no more texts. I walk out to my bike and strap my stuff on the rack. He doesn't say not to come. I text Judith that I'll be late for work.

———

Connor opens the door.

"Here's my ticket." I hand him the short roll of Double Stuf Oreos I picked up at the gas station snack rack on the corner. It's the regular kind he always preferred, not any of the other weird flavors or colors.

"Thanks."

In the kitchen, I decline his offer of milk and he pours himself a glass. He opens the Oreos, sticks a fork deep into the white cream of one, and lowers it into his milk. I'd forgotten about that little trick of his.

"I'm sorry," I say.

"Wasn't your fault. Besides, Annie and I weren't friends."

"What do you mean? Did you have a fight?"

"We were never friends. You thought we were?"

Thinking about it now, of course they weren't. They were pulled together by Zumi. Like I was. Annie wanted us all to be like planets in her orbit, but Zumi was actually the sun in our group.

I shrug. "We never talked about it."

He holds the Oreos out to me. "Have some."

I shake my head. I know he loves them and it's a small package.

"Go on. Scientifically engineered to taste awesome."

He has a point. More importantly, Dr. Jordan taught me that sometimes refusing a gift is the same as rejecting the giver.

"Can I have a fork?"

He gives me one and we go out to sit on the long couch like old times, at opposite ends with our legs outstretched. His feet rest entirely on the cushions while mine dangle at the ankle.

As I finish my last cookie, it occurs to me I jumped a little quickly to the idea that Connor was tolerating Annie for Zumi's sake. Maybe there was more to it. I pick up one of the throw pillows to have something to do with my hands. "Can I ask you a question?"

He grabs his phone, taps the screen, and holds it out. I see the last thing I texted him:

> **I'm not coming to ask you anything.**

I laugh. "Okay. I meant about Annie or Zumi, but if you want to hold me to it..."

"For someone with a lawyer for a dad, you aren't careful with words."

"I'm not careful with lots of things. That's why I didn't want my own glass of milk."

He chuckles.

I have at least three clear memories of my fifteen-year-old arm sweeping grandly in his kitchen and knocking over full glasses, shattering at least one.

"You'd think your mom would've stopped offering me drinks. But it seemed like it didn't bother her."

"She said..." He shakes his head. "Never mind."

"What?" I ask. When he doesn't answer, I say, "You can't... You have to tell me now."

"She said the world needs more girls who don't keep their hands in their laps."

"She didn't say that...."

Connor shrugs. He finishes off the rest of his milk.

I say, "I saw you hanging out with Annie sometimes when Zumi wasn't around."

"Zumi wanted us all to be friends."

"You sure you didn't like her? Annie?"

He glances at me. Briefly, but it's more than usual.

"You know what I mean," I say.

"I was just going along. For Zumi."

We've never talked about this. Now with Annie gone and Zumi shut down, I think maybe we can.

"Do you like Zumi?"

He smiles. "Are you trying to say I have girl friends because I want a girlfriend but can't get out of the friend zone?"

"I'm not saying. I'm asking. You were in a clique of girls. I was last to join and first to leave. If you had a crush on someone, it wasn't me."

"Nothing personal. I'm looking for a girl who keeps her hands in her lap."

"Hey!" I throw the pillow at him. He ducks it and grabs the other pillow before I can. He crosses his arms over it.

"Fine," I say. "You didn't answer me."

"God, Mel, she's like my sister. Maybe that happens when you can still remember making mud pies together in preschool."

"That's still not a *no*."

He holds up a hand. "I solemnly swear I don't have a crush on Zumi, *or* Annie, *or* you, no offense." He drops his hand. "What about you?"

I laugh and raise my hand. "I solemnly swear I don't have a crush on you, either."

He smirks. "Not on *me* ..."

I peer at him. "Are you ... are you saying you think *I'm* ...?"

"Not saying. Asking."

"Oh. I'm straight."

"Same here."

I tip my head, watching his face to see his reaction, and say, "Zumi's not."

He just nods.

"She ever tell you?" I ask.

"No. We've never talked about it."

I guess he just strongly suspects, then. Same as me.

"Annie, too—" I hear myself say before I can stop.

"Annie?" he says sharply. "I thought she was straight. She talked that way, at least."

A spike of adrenaline burns through me.

"Mel, what did she tell you?"

I take a deep breath and let it out, trying to cool down. "What'd she say we fought about?"

"She said you made fun of us behind our backs until one day she had enough. She told us what you supposedly said, about Zumi being clumsy and crude, and me being a creepy hermit."

"Supposedly? You didn't believe her?"

"I hardly believed anything Annie said. Besides, it all sounded like stuff *she* would say. Didn't sound like you. But we didn't see you anymore, so it didn't matter much."

"Zumi believed her."

Connor grimaces. "Yeah, it got to her. Especially when you didn't defend yourself."

I look down at my hands.

He says, "I told myself I wasn't going to ask, but ... why

didn't you answer our texts and...I mean, I've never had mono but it couldn't have been *that* bad."

"I was pretty sick," I say. "But I also didn't want you guys caught in the middle of me and Annie."

"So what did you two really fight about?"

I shrug. "Take her story and switch the names around, for a start."

"I suspected that much," he says. "What else?"

"We also fought because I found out Annie liked girls—"

"Wait, you didn't just suspect—she actually told you?"

I nod. It was unmistakable.

He closes his eyes and tips his head back to face the ceiling. "Shit."

"Yeah. Then I asked if she knew Zumi had a crush on her. She said of course, but that it would never happen. Which...which was fine. Everyone has a right to like who they want. But I...I called her out on how she led Zumi on. Then whenever Zumi started looking too hopeful, Annie would push her away and rave about some guy in a movie or magazine to throw her off. I couldn't talk to anyone about this stuff to see if I was imagining it, so I just kept it bottled up. When Annie flat out admitted it, I...I just kind of lost it."

Connor looks down again. "That's why you stopped talking to us. You couldn't explain what happened without Zumi hearing all that."

I nod. "I never understood why Zumi loved Annie, but that doesn't matter. Why does anybody love anybody? I guess I was a coward. If I was a good friend, I'd have told her."

Connor reaches out and pulls my dangling feet up to rest solidly on the sofa cushion. "She wouldn't have believed you."

"A good friend would have tried anyway."

"I guess I'm a bad friend, too," Connor says. "I didn't know everything you knew, but I knew Annie didn't treat her well. I could see Zumi stung by it sometimes, but mostly she was happy around Annie even without them being together. I don't think people have the right to interfere with anyone else's relationships, even if it's with someone you think is no good. We wouldn't want Zumi meddling with who *we* like."

I smile. "Except she would anyway."

"Okay." He smiles back. "Bad example."

FOURTEEN

Hamster is *RUNNING*

Hummingbird is *HOVERING*

Hammerhead is *CRUISING*

Hanniganimal is *LEVEL*

We're supposed to finish our Chem lab reports and submit them online today, only something's wrong with the Web portal. Next week is spring break but Mr. Gottfried doesn't want to put it off that long. He tells us to send everything in from home by Sunday night. This makes me think about the assignments Zumi's missing. Mr. Gottfried says no one's picked up any work for her, so I do.

I text Connor to meet me at lunch. He knows Zumi's schedule, and we go room to room picking up her assignments. It strikes me as odd that he hasn't been doing this but he says she told him not to. I'm surprised he didn't just do it anyway. I think he's more out of sorts than he's admitting. It's the push I need to decide to do it myself.

When school lets out, I ask Holly for a ride.

"Really?" she says.

"I have Zumi's textbooks and can't carry everything on my bike."

"Oh."

"You talking to her now?" Declan asks.

"Nope." I don't know what else to say.

I get everything organized while Holly brings the car around. They help cram everything into the backseat, bike and me included.

Fifteen minutes later, everything is piled on the curb in front of Zumi's house.

"Mel," Holly says. "You know what you're doing?"

"Nope."

Holly looks at me for a moment. Then she nods. "Call me if you need anything." She drives away.

It takes two trips to shuttle everything to Zumi's porch. I strap my stuff to the bike rack so I'm ready to hop on and ride away when the time comes. I take it slow, trying to work out what I'll say, but it all depends on Zumi. And if she won't say anything, she also won't stand around to listen to any prepared speeches.

I gather up her books and binders and knock on the door.

It opens. Zumi's in her usual faded jeans, sneakers, and her black DON'T ASK hoodie.

"I brought your books and stuff. And the assignments you missed."

Her eyelids look like balloons that got blown up, stretched to the limit, and then emptied again. They're not red, though. She just looks exhausted.

Seeing her books seems to alarm her. She glances left and right. "Where's Connor?"

"I don't know. He didn't bring me."

"How'd you get in my locker?"

"Oh, he just opened it—he didn't tell me your combination." I swallow. "He's worried about you. *I'm* worried about you. Is there anything I can do?"

"Just leave it."

She closes the door.

I set her books and binders down on the porch bench, up against the armrest nearest the door. I sit next to them. I don't want to leave her like this.

My hand reaches out to a dark stain on the bench. When we were fourteen, Zumi put a pumpkin here. Her brother Eddie carved it to look like Jack Skellington from *The Nightmare Before Christmas*. Zumi loved it so much she wouldn't let anyone touch it after Halloween ended. A week later it collapsed into a puddle of furry goo and she still blocked any cleanup. It surprised me her parents went along—it was gross and probably toxic—and over many months it shrunk, dried, hardened, and eroded away, finally leaving only this stain.

The door opens. I'm not sure how long I've been here.

"You can go." Zumi's voice is flat.

"Do you want me to?"

She doesn't answer.

I scoot over on the bench to make room for her.

She hesitates, and then she picks up her books.

"Mom went to Santa Cruz to get Eddie. Next week is his

spring break, too. They'll be here any minute." She heads back into the house.

I don't know what Zumi's family thinks about why I don't come around anymore. I stand and lean over toward the doorway. "Can I come back tomorrow?"

She glances at me and closes the door.

She didn't say *no*.

———

Dr. Oswald called to tell me she couldn't get to her office in time for our session. She works clinic hours on Fridays and it's sometimes hard to get away. We arranged to start meeting on Mondays instead. It surprised me that I felt a little disappointed about not seeing her today. In her honor, after dinner, I got a game of Hold'em going at the Silver Sands.

I told Dr. Jordan we'd fleece Dr. Oswald in poker, but really I meant *he* could. So could anyone else at the table: Mr. Terrance Knight, even the new additions, Ms. Li and David. I have a decent poker face but a terrible poker body.

Good cards push adrenaline into my blood. It accelerates my breathing, which I can sort of fix, but it also makes my hands shake. Since I can't stop these tremors, and I can't fake them to bluff with bad cards, it's pretty much hopeless.

The cards I have now add a new symptom: sweat. It doesn't make sense, really. We're only playing for chips. I don't even have a good hand, just a remote possibility...but still...

Mr. Terrance Knight dealt me the five and seven of clubs

and I called, hoping for a flush. A novice move, but it's just for fun. Next came another club, the nine, and then the six of clubs. That's when the trembling began, plus sweating around my temples. I still have nothing, and the odds that the last card will give me the club flush are still low, and the odds I'll get the straight are tiny...but you can't reason with adrenaline.

Mr. Terrance Knight dominates, like in every game we play. Ms. Li and Dr. Jordan fold, leaving me and David. We both call Mr. Terrance Knight's bet.

He deals—holy shit—the *eight of clubs*, filling my odds-defying five-nine straight flush! I guess I was only perspiring before—*now* I'm sweating.

Mr. Terrance Knight bets big. I'd be happy to take the pot as is. Might as well go all the way, since...I stare at the community cards...there's literally no way I can lose.

"All in."

David exhales loudly and tosses down his cards.

Mr. Terrance Knight watches me stoically. I can't hide that I have a good hand....Maybe if I ham it up, he'll think I'm trying to make it out better than it is.

I grin. "You should probably fold."

He watches me, uncharacteristically stony—his poker face. Then he drops his cards on the pile.

"Damn it!" I cry. "Where's your gumption?"

Mr. Terrance Knight smiles and starts collecting the discards. "Gumption's a ticket to the poorhouse."

"What'd you have?" David asks me.

I grab my cards to show my triumph but Mr. Terrance

Knight catches my eye. In real poker, when everyone else folds, your cards are like a magician's secrets, never to be revealed.

But this hand's too good! A rare and wondrous thing!

Damn it.

I slide my cards into the pile. "Guess you should've paid to see 'em."

"Sha-ZAM!" Mr. Terrance Knight laughs. "Our little Mel is growin' up!"

Ms. Li's eyes crinkle.

———

Not surprisingly, I'm first out. I move to the couch and obey the rules of when to talk and not talk, and what to say and what not to say when out of the game. From here I can see David's cards, and it doesn't take me long to figure out his tell. He runs his fingers through the hair above his forehead when he's bluffing. I think Mr. Terrance Knight figured it out, too, because he always calls David's bluffs, and soon David's also out of the game.

When he stands, Ms. Li presses something into his hand.

"Take her to dinner."

The fact that she doesn't need to say my name makes my skin flush.

"We...already ate," David says.

"You had salads. Time for a main course."

There was a "soy loaf" option at dinner but it looked like something you'd find in a petting zoo feeding trough. The real meat loaf looked good but I skipped it and made a salad.

119

Not to pretend I'd turned vegetarian; I just saw David's nose twitch and thought I'd spare him the smell.

I check my phone, partly to hide my face. "It's eight o'clock."

"Olive Garden's open till ten," Ms. Li says. "I recommend the manicotti."

Mr. Terrance Knight tries to suppress a grin. Dr. Jordan hides behind his mug of tea.

David looks to me again, noticeably self-conscious. "Are you even hungry?"

There are two ways to get through this awkward scene: slowly peel off the Band-Aid, or . . .

"Starving." I jump to my feet. "And I love manicotti."

He grins wryly and tries to give back the folded bills. "I don't need money."

"Go!" she says. "So we can do proper buy-ins and stop playing for plastic like children! Don't hurry back. I need concentration to take down Iron Face." She gestures vaguely toward Mr. Terrance Knight and this segues into waving David away. "Go!"

It didn't take long for Ms. Li to settle in. I see again where David gets his disdain for preliminaries and formality. I lead him outside.

"Thanks," he says. "You really are starving, aren't you? If you could bluff that convincingly, we'd still be in the game."

We? Did he throw the game to get out right after me?

"Yep," I say. "Genuinely starving. You must be, too. Your salad was weak. But I was just helping you out in there. Don't feel obligated."

"Oh...so..." he says. "Do you want to go, or...?"

I feel bad—I guess I'm giving mixed signals. But I do have mixed feelings. I like him, but I can't imagine letting him get close enough to qualify as a boyfriend.

Not to get ahead of myself. It's just dinner.

"No—I mean *yes*, I do want to." I point at myself. "Starving, remember? What about you?"

He smiles. "Also starving. And she won't let me give the money back. *And* it wouldn't be right to use it for anything else."

I wince. "Olive Garden?"

"Only if you want to." He retrieves keys from his pocket. "I'll eat anywhere you pick as long as it's not some place called Meat, Meat, Only Meat. My tank's almost empty. Am I going to need gas?"

I shake my head. "You won't even need keys."

FIFTEEN

Hamster is *Running*

Hummingbird is *Flying*

Hammerhead is *Cruising*

Hanniganimal is *Up!*

We walk back from Thai Fu Son along the beach trail, full of noodles and sushi. The dunes to the right block our view of the highway but not the sound. The white noise of cars is not much different from crashing surf; it'd be hard to guess our direction with closed eyes. Without a moon, all we have are foot lamps to give us enough light to stay on the path and out of the sand.

David says, "You're in a good mood today."

This makes me smile. I bet he doesn't track my moods like I do.

"Any particular reason?" he asks. "Or just glad it's Friday?"

"You fishing for a compliment?"

"Hardly. You were already charged up when I got there, singing more than usual—"

"Sorry."

"—and getting that game started. You were bouncing around before any of my witty dinner conversation or buying you Asian fusion."

I smile again, though it's dark enough he might not be able to see it.

"In case you didn't realize it," he says, "that place represented just about every Asian tradition except mine. I felt left out."

"We got fortune cookies."

"Those aren't really Chinese."

"Neither are you. You're more American than I am. All my great-grandparents came from England and Europe. Your grandmother said your family's been in or around San Francisco for five generations, and that's where fortune cookies were invented. Your heritage was not only represented, it was the most authentic part of the meal. Those Thai noodles we had probably were nothing like they'd really be in Thailand."

"Wow. You suck at poker but you'd be great on the debate team. You said your dad's a lawyer. You want to be?"

"No. I'm only convincing if I don't have to lie."

We walk on. I'm not sure why this is the moment we're silent.

"So you've never lied to me?" David asks playfully.

My heart sinks. Telling him at dinner that I had no siblings wasn't *technically* a lie. Maybe I only get tremors when I'm dishonest in trivial ways.

123

I think he's just kidding around, but I can't see his face well enough to be sure. I stop walking. "Put out your hands, faceup."

"Why?"

"It's too dark to see if mine are shaking. You have to feel it."

He complies. I hold my hands over his, palms barely touching.

"You're shaking," he says.

"Doesn't count yet. It's cold." Plus now I have adrenaline running through my body for a different reason. "And you saw me before. I shake more than this when bluffing at poker. Now, ask me a question that's hard to answer truthfully."

"Hmmm...Let me think...."

"Don't hurt yourself."

"Okay, got one. Have you ever had sex?"

"David!" I laugh and yank my hands away. "What kind of question is that!"

"It's perfect," he says, grinning like he'd outmaneuvered me, which he had. "It's hard to tell the truth about that, no matter what the answer is."

He looks into my eyes, not wavering, but not provoking or intruding. Many people, even when they're not checking their phones or looking over your shoulder, aren't completely present. When David talks to me, he's always *here*.

It feels wonderful, but also mixed. Like having fun playing in the surf interrupted by bursts of a sudden fear of drowning.

But I have to answer his question. At least I want to, as much as I can. I put my hands gently back on his. I'm shaking more but he doesn't say anything. Maybe I can fight fire with fire.

"I have never had sex," I say in a quiet voice, watching his eyes. "*If* . . . and I mean *if* . . . when you say *sex* . . . you mean a *penis* entering my *vagina*."

David laughs and drops his hands.

"Was I lying?"

"I can't know for sure," he says. "But I believe you, and that was the point."

"What about you?"

"I never said *I* had to answer any hard questions."

"I didn't have to, either."

"Okay," he says. "Sticking with your narrow and somewhat unimaginative definition of sex—"

"Hey!"

"—I've also never had sex before."

"Whoa, whoa, wait a minute . . . sticking with *my* definition? A penis has never entered your vagina?"

He laughs again. "You're definitely going to be a lawyer. Lawyers don't have to lie to be convincing. They just have to ask the right questions."

We resume walking. I stuff my hands in my pockets.

"Ever had a girlfriend?" I ask. That's a normal question for friends to ask each other. "Not a girl who's a friend. A *girl-friend*, like, with the mushy stuff."

"Dates, valentines, sure. Getting round the bases, not so much."

"Why not?"

125

"You'd have to ask them. I've never broken up with any-one. Been on the receiving end twice. For the same reason, so it must be true."

"Which was?"

"They both said I'm too intense."

"Ooooooh…" I fake a shiver as a joke. Inside I feel a real one. What drove those other girls away is what's trying to reel me in.

"Have you had any?" he asks.

I look at him pointedly.

"*Boy*friends, I mean."

"No."

"But you've dated before this?"

"Is this a date?"

"Um… I thought so… unless—"

"It started out with your *grandma* giving you money to get us out of her way. And you sounded reluctant."

"That… that was something else…."

"It seemed *reluctant* to me."

"I'd just wanted to ask you myself. Not have anyone else set us up and pay."

I stop walking. It was easy to act like we were out as friends before, but it's not ambiguous anymore, not unless I say otherwise right now. Or at least pretty soon.

"When did you want to ask me out? You didn't even like me at first."

"I liked the *look* of you from the start," David says, and I shiver again. "I just wanted her to move in with us, not have… strangers take care of her."

126

"I know." I catch myself swaying and force it to stop. "So what made you decide to ask me out?"

"Well..." He thinks a moment. "Four things did it."

"Four! Okay, what was first?"

"You laughed when I called you a terrible singer."

I laugh again. "It's true. Second thing?"

"I saw how you were with everyone there, not just with my grandma. Like it's not work at all."

"It's not."

"I know. Third thing is...don't laugh, but...brown hair, blue eyes, freckles...those are all on my bucket list. You're one-stop shopping—"

"What?!" I swat his shoulder. "I'm some kind of *package deal*?"

He laughs.

"You're just making stuff up," I say. I count on my fingers. "So far I'm nice, a bad singer, and conform to random open check boxes on your Achievements List....Number four better be good, if there even *is* a number four."

"Grandma says when you find someone, you need to feel two things in particular or else it's doomed."

I brace myself, afraid to guess.

"She says you need fondness and fire, in large, equal amounts. Then there's a chance."

I search his eyes for any sign of bullshit....

"What are you thinking?" he asks.

"Generally?" It comes out hoarse. I clear my throat. "Or is this one of those questions where it's hard to tell the truth?"

127

Adrenaline isn't seeping into my blood—it's an injection. I clench my trembling hands in my pockets.

"Your choice," he says.

"Okay...I'm thinking..."

Oh, what the hell. Kissing someone doesn't mean signing a contract to reveal everything about me.

I take a deep breath and let it out.

"First base, definitely," I say with a firm nod. "Second base is a maybe. I'm not sure what third base is....I've heard different definitions. Probably shouldn't hit all the bases the first night, anyway."

He grins and looks down. Why? He doesn't usually look away.

"We're not going to hit *any* bases tonight," he says. "And your lie detector test is the closest we're getting to holding hands."

Oh God...when he said *fondness*...did he mean...? But he said *fire*...or does he think fire means something else? What else could it mean? Wait, he said that's what Ms. Li said, not what he actually felt. And I'm afraid to go too far with this, anyway, so why is my heart plummeting?

"Hey." He lowers his head and frowns. "I just don't want to scare you off. You know, being too intense."

He has no idea. If anyone's going to get scared off, it's him. Just as well. This wasn't going to go far anyway.

I shrug. "I'm not like other girls."

He laughs. "That's what they all say. I also don't want it to be on someone else's dime, or have it be anyone else's idea."

I think back to the poker table as we got bundled off. I can see those smiles turning smug if we come back holding hands.

"Yeah, you're right," I say. "In fact, this wasn't even a date. It was a *pre-date*. Next time can be our first official date. Don't want them taking credit for what we were already thinking."

David grins.

Damn it—why the hell did I say *we*?

SIXTEEN

Hamster is STUMBLING

Hummingbird is PERCHED

Hammerhead is THRASHING*

Hanniganimal is DOWN

Running on the beach, feet sinking in sand, heart pounding, losing ground, queasy, gasping from exertion and rising panic, doubling over from stabbing pains—

A dream: hazy, fading, details lost…but the nausea is real. So is the pain, though it's lower down. It's unquestionably a shark attack. A bad one.

Instantly awake, I waddle down the hall. Damn, it got on my nightshirt, my favorite with the zombie teddy bears. Oh, wait, that's not real blood, just part of the design. Phew.

I skulk back to my room, shivering. Clean underwear, sweats, socks—a pause to take my morning meds plus ibuprofen, no Ritalin—and I crawl back under the covers.

This wasn't due till Monday. I try to look on the bright side; after a promising visit with Zumi and a fun dinner out with David, I forgot to set my alarm and would've slept past time for my meds if the shark bite hadn't woken me up. I'm also glad Dad's out of town again so I can hole up here all weekend.

But now, even skipping the Ritalin, I can't imagine falling back asleep.

I fade in and out all morning, waking up for the umpteenth time: sweaty, bleary, confused. Every time I thought I wouldn't be able to fall back asleep, I did. Now the sun is high outside the window.

The queasiness is gone but I'm not fooled; it'll be back. The pain dimmed, too, but that was the pills and it's already returning. I need more ibuprofen but I'm out of water, and I don't want to dry swallow, yet I really don't want to move. As long as I stay here in my cocoon, time might stand still.

It doesn't. The pain surges, but that's not what'll get me out of bed. Shark attack plus skipping Ritalin plus no breakfast adds up to ravenous hunger. I check my phone; it's almost one thirty. No missed calls or texts. I slowly unwrap, get up, and slump down the hall.

Mom's at the stove frying two eggs in the iron skillet. She's wearing her overalls so I won't be able to. She lifts the lid on a quart saucepan to show me steaming-hot mac and cheese.

I wrap my arms around her.

"Hey," she says. "I've got to get these out if you want runny yolk."

I free her arms and put my head on her shoulder. "Best Mom Ever."

"Jesus, Mel." HJ walks in. "You're not going to cry, are you? That's so cliché."

"How soon they forget," Mom says and slides the eggs onto a plate. "*Somebody* must not remember how this cheesy egg recipe got invented in the first place. And back then you'd think the world was coming to an end every full moon."

HJ rolls her eyes without answering. She opens the fridge.

"You want to do the honor?" Mom swings the saucepan handle toward me.

I nod and pour the whole batch of cheesy noodles over the eggs. I grab a fork and sit with my plate at the table. The toaster pops. Aunt Joan sits across from me and sets down a ginormous glass of milk, followed by a bottle of ibuprofen, and slides them over. Mom brings two slices of toast, each glistening with enough butter to qualify as frosting.

"God, that's revolting." HJ reaches forward. "Especially this—"

I hunch and growl, fork out like a weapon.

"Easy!" She pulls back. "I wasn't...Okay, I was. I guess you need it more than me."

I take some tablets with a big slug of milk, and then I dig in.

HJ glances at Mom and says, "Pats here tells me you went on a date! How'd it go?"

"Fine," I say. With a full mouth, it comes out like *fawn*.

"Fine? What'd you do?"

"Dinner. Thai Fu Son."

"That's not how this works, Mel. What happened? Paint a picture!"

I swallow, resigning myself to speaking complete sentences, or at least more words. "Walking. Eating. No sweaty car sex. No groping, no tongues, no holding hands. No moon over the beach. No getting caught in the rain. Not even a good-night kiss."

"You sure it was a date?"

"Joanie..." Mom warns.

"I'm being serious. You go out with friends sometimes. If you didn't do anything friends wouldn't do, what made it a date?"

"We said it was." I'm not going to explain how we decided it was a *pre-date*.

"All right." HJ nods. "The shy ones don't always kiss you the first time."

I guess by this answer, and HJ's eyes, and the pause in the noisy cleanup behind me, that Mom's probably glaring at her. The clatter resumes.

"So you like him? He going to ask you out again?"

I close my eyes. "I'm not a mind reader." I open them again. "We said we'd do it again."

"You set up something specific? Sometimes they say that but—"

"Joanie..." Mom warns again.

"We didn't but we're going to. If he doesn't bring it up soon, I will."

"Well, don't need to go that far—"

"Joan," Mom says. "Stop."

"I'm just saying—"

"Stop. Talking."

She does. I keep my face down and concentrate on shoveling in food.

HJ comes around the table. She wraps her long bony arms around me and pushes her cheek against mine, both of us facing my messy plate.

"I love you, Mel."

She lets go and kisses my head. "I've got to put in a few hours. The good part about working on Saturday is wearing jeans to the office. Jeans are my best feature."

By the time HJ is out the door, I don't hear Mom in the kitchen. I finish eating and can think of nothing except how I want to cocoon up and wait for the world to spin around a few more times before I come out again.

Mom appears and takes my dishes. "I made up your bed. I also got your laundry out so I won't have to go in there again this afternoon."

"Thanks." I stand.

"Did you have a nice time last night?"

I nod.

"Good." She puts my dishes in the sink and turns on the faucet. "You know she just worries about you."

I head down the hall.

"I worry about her, too."

———

My moods are beyond frustrating, especially when they directly *contradict* reason. Period hormones can trigger mood

134

swings and push my symptoms especially hard, but so does regular old stress. Not just the bad kind, either. Dr. Jordan told me bipolar disorder doesn't distinguish between anxiety and excitement. The cruel irony is how this can add up to feeling nothing but dark clouds *because* things went well yesterday.

No holding hands, no good-night kiss, and he said *fondness*. He said other things, but maybe he was just being nice. Do we have a connection or don't we? Am I just seeing what I want to see? The only reason you recognize yourself in a horoscope is that you can see what you want anywhere if you look hard enough.

We exchanged numbers but I haven't heard from him. God, it was only last night; why would he call this soon? It would be nice if he did, though. I wish he would. I could always text him—except HJ would kill me if she found out I texted a guy first.

And where's the girl who wanted to push back last night, to keep him far enough away to protect both of us? Or here's a better question: Which girl is the real me?

And with Zumi, I got excited as I pedaled away from her house, but all I had was asking if I could come back and she closed the door on me—

No! The good things yesterday, I didn't imagine them. This paranoia, *this* isn't real. My imagination is spinning its wheels, questioning everything that's no longer right in front of me proving itself real.

I can think clearly enough to know that second-guessing everything now is just chickenshit bipolar shenanigans. Yet knowing this still doesn't stop me from feeling like a freshman again, carrying my lunch tray past Annie, Zumi, and Connor, afraid they've forgotten me, or that our first conversation hadn't meant what I thought—

Damn it, stop! These tears running down my nose, puddling on my pillow, with this feeling that the world outside is running smoothly without me, doesn't need me, doesn't want me, doesn't even know I'm here...none of that's real. It's just chemicals—

A soft knock at the door makes me jump. "Mel?"

Tears have turned into audible crying. This happens sometimes on first days for no other reason, so I hope she doesn't suspect there's more to it this time.

"I'm fine," I say. I don't sound fine.

"Let me know if you need anything."

I need to stop thinking. It'll just get worse. I grab the Ativan and shake out a couple tabs. Mom refilled my water bottle and I slug them down, but it'll take time for them to work. *If* they work. Sometimes they aren't enough to pull me down when I'm ramping up.

Zumi didn't just close the door. It was how she glanced at me, her eyes slack, not squinted. Everything about her said *yes*, I could come back tomorrow—

Wait...not tomorrow. *Today.*

I'm in no state to do it now. But I can't flake on her. She's broken over her best friend—also her crush—completely abandoning her after years of being together every day, and I got my period—it doesn't rate. Only there's no denying I wouldn't be any good to her now. I might even make things worse. I have to put this off in some way that doesn't seem like I'm bailing on her.

I get my phone. After typing countless trivial variations, I send her a text.

> Feel shitty. Come tomorrow
> instead?

I'm not sure what I'll do if she doesn't answer. Luckily I don't have to think about it long.

> **No. Everyone back by 5
> and here all day tomorrow.**

I get another text almost right away:

> **Don't come if you're sick. I
> don't want to catch it.**

This means she did want me to come. And she still does, even though she's not asking. Or she'd tell me not to. Definitely. Maybe.

> Not contagious. See you in
> an hour.

SEVENTEEN

Hamster is STUMBLING

Hummingbird is PERCHED

Hammerhead is THRASHING*

Hanniganimal is DOWN

Zumi's house is only a ten-minute ride away but I don't feel like sitting on my bike. I also want to give the Ativan more time to kick in.

After walking a few blocks, it occurs to me that among countless trips to Zumi's, this is only the second time I've gone on foot. It's fitting because that other time was when we argued and then stopped talking.

It was also a Saturday like today. I walked because Mom had taken away my bike the night before and put it in her bedroom. That's actually what gave me the idea of parking it routinely in the house. It never occurred to me before that it didn't have to stay in the garage.

Mom had been secretly checking my odometer—for the same reason she'd made Nolan put it on the bike, I later learned—to make sure I was only riding to and from school and around the neighborhood. This particular Friday night she demanded to know how I'd managed to put on over forty miles that day. I was taken so much by surprise, by her knowing and by the angry fear in her voice, I told the truth. After school I had biked twenty miles up the Great Highway to the Golden Gate Bridge.

Mom completely lost it: yelling, crying. It scared me so much that I didn't tell her the rest. How I hadn't turned off my light the night before and was going on thirty-six hours without getting sleepy for the first time in my life. About the big fight I had with Annie right after school that day, and how afterward my heart rate shot up over a thousand and I thought my head was going to explode from panic. I had to let the energy out somehow, so I pedaled as fast as I could to the one place within reach where I have calm, happy memories of Nolan with nothing bad mixed in. When I reached the bridge my heart was pounding hard but slower. I sat against the south tower in our special spot till I calmed down some more. Then I rode back home.

I stayed up again all that Friday night, approaching fifty hours awake, and snuck out of the house the next morning to walk to Zumi's. I'd spent that entire second sleepless night plotting how we could stay friends and I had to get to her before Annie did.

I knocked on the Shimuras' door, oblivious to the fact that seven thirty on a Saturday morning was way too early to be here. Luckily I'd become a common presence and Zumi's dad was already headed out; he often worked weekends on rental properties he owned. He frowned while he shuttled me to Zumi's room, telling me to be quiet since Zumi's mom was still asleep.

————

I sit on the edge of Zumi's bed. She doesn't wake up. I bounce. I whisper her name. Louder. I put a hand on her shoulder and rock her.

Her eyes open, bleary.

"Mel? What's going on?"

Where are all my plans from last night? I guess I was just thinking around and around what I wanted: to stay friends with Zumi. That means she has to break away from Annie, too, but a voice in my head keeps saying that's never going to happen.

"Annie and I aren't friends anymore."

"I know, she told me last night." Zumi sits up and rubs her eyes. She's wearing the "love pirate" pajamas I gave her on her last birthday: cutlasses, arrow-pierced hearts, and Jolly Rogers. "Where were you all afternoon?"

"I ... I rode up to the Golden Gate Bridge."

"No you didn't."

"It took hours. And I had to walk here since my mom took away my bike. What'd Annie tell you?"

"Why've you been so weird? Ever since I got back from Thanksgiving. And hard to find. Annie, too. What's going on?"

"You were away at your grandma's. I got tired of Annie being such a bitch—"

"Annie's not—"

140

"She is! She always has to have everything her way. She treats Connor like dirt."

"He doesn't care."

"That doesn't make it okay! She's mean and treats you like dirt, too."

"No she doesn't. What's gotten into you—"

"I just don't want us doing what she says all the time!"

"I don't do whatever she—".

"You do! Tell me one time you didn't."

"I…"

"See, you can't! You always do what she says."

"I just like the same things. She doesn't order me around like Connor."

"See, you just said it! She says what she wants and if we don't do it, she…she picks at us, saying little bitchy things till we do."

Zumi shakes her head. She won't look at me.

I feel her slipping away. "Did Annie tell you not to talk to me?"

Zumi rolls her eyes and groans. She pulls her knees up and drops her head down on them and disappears behind her hair.

"She did, didn't she?"

She doesn't answer.

"Look at me, Zumi! Look at me!"

She doesn't.

"You're…you're my best friend! How can you believe her instead of me?"

"She's my best friend."

My heart stops.

"Zumi, I…I…I…" I can't talk straight anymore. And it's not just my tongue—it's like my brain is stuttering.

141

"She said you've been going behind my back. That you were glad I was finally the one gone for a week this time." She lifts her head and looks at me. "Were you?"

I want to shout NO! but I can't. It feels like a hand is squeezing my throat. I shake my head.

"Say it, Mel," she whispers. I've never heard her sound like this before, like she's pleading. "Look me in the eye and tell me you didn't say those things."

I can't speak. I can't even breathe. I'm getting dizzy. All I can do is shake my head harder and it makes me dizzier.

Her face pinches and she drops her nose to her knees again.

"I don't get it. Everything was so great."

I reach out for her arm—

The door swings open. Standing there is Zumi's mom in a dark red robe.

"Zumi? What's Mel doing here? Why is she crying?"

I leap off the bed. Zumi's mom tries to stop me—I dodge and run down the hall.

"Mel!" she calls. "Honey, wait!"

I yank open the door and run outside, over the porch, across the lawn, down the street....

———

Four hours later I was in a hospital. The kind where everyone's in chairs instead of beds.

I'd been ramping up since Thanksgiving. Dr. Jordan later said he'd seen me acting strange and was keeping an eye on me, and when I didn't show up at the Silver Sands that Friday afternoon, he told Grandma Cece, and she told Mom, that I probably had bipolar disorder. Like HJ. Like Nolan.

That's what Mom had just heard when she found out I'd ridden my bike alone twenty miles up the Great Highway to the Suicide Capital of the World.

Then that Saturday morning, when I burst into the house after running home from Zumi's, Mom was on the phone in a panic. Zumi's mom had called and now Mom was calling everyone else we knew, looking for me, and was about to call the police. That solo run was the last time I got to be alone for more than a year.

In those awful weeks, and then months—getting my diagnosis, seeing doctors, trying all kinds of meds, missing school, making up illnesses, hiding from Zumi, trying to catch up on schoolwork—that morning at Zumi's house just got further and further away. Then it was too late. Holly still thinks Zumi abandoned me when I got sick, but really it was the other way around.

Walking back to Zumi's now, it feels like I'm about to finish the conversation I ran away from sixteen months ago, only this time with the help of so much medical science running through my veins and brain.

Yet when I reach Zumi's house, the Ativan is helping but I'm still not ready to knock. I sit down on the bench and put my hand on the mark left by Eddie's jack-o'-lantern again.

The door opens.

I'm afraid to look up. I'm here to help Zumi. To try and patch things up. But I'm feeling fragile and unbalanced.

"Why are you here?" It's not an accusation. She sounds confused.

"I want to help."

"Why?"

I think a moment. Then I say, "Because I'm your friend."

"Huh. Is that why you disappeared on me? And wouldn't answer my texts. Or my calls. Or the *door*?"

"I was really sick."

She blows air through her nose. "You couldn't have been *that* sick."

I don't say anything.

"All those things Annie said, about how you were tired of me, because you thought I was...obnoxious...I didn't believe her at first."

I look up. Zumi's standing on the mat, one hand on the doorjamb.

"You thought she was lying?"

"Was she?"

I nod.

"I thought so. But then you kept avoiding me. I finally had to believe her. I even apologized for calling her a liar."

"Sorry. I...I was sick, and I...You said she was your best friend. With me and her fighting, you couldn't stay friends with us both. I just thought it was better to..."

"To what? Act like a twelve-year-old? Be a martyr?"

"And a coward. I'm sorry."

Zumi sighs. "Stop saying that. I get it. You being sorry, I mean."

144

She sits on the bench a couple feet away.

I say, "Can you forgive me?"

"Maybe. Forgetting is harder."

I'll take what I can get.

"If you had to do it over again," she says, "what would you do different?"

The question surprises me. I have no idea how to answer it.

Her phone chirps. She checks it.

"They're coming back early. Be here in a few minutes."

She stands and walks to the front door.

"Zumi?"

She pauses but doesn't look back.

I swallow. "I wish a lot was different."

She nods and goes back in the house.

EIGHTEEN

Hamster is STUMBLING

Hummingbird is PERCHED

Hammerhead is THRASHING*

Hanniganimal is DOWN

After I leave Zumi's I get a text from Judith asking if I'm okay. It takes a moment to realize I'm an hour late for work. Judith is very flexible about my schedule but it's also possible she only just noticed I wasn't there. I'm less than two miles from the Silver Sands. I walk over.

I change, wash, and look for Ms. Arguello to see if someone already got her juice. I find her alone in the Sun Room, an empty glass on the table by her elbow. She's balling yarn, no scarf visible anywhere. She must have just finished one.

"Hi, Ms. Arguello. May I sit with you?"

"Of course, dear. Is this your first day? How do you know my name?"

"Judith told me." I sit on the sofa, her satchel of yarn between us.

"Are you a nurse?"

"No, I just help out. My name's Mel Hannigan."

"Mel? For Melissa? Or Melinda?"

"Just Mel."

She sets aside a finished ball of canary yellow and picks up a skein of rust-colored yarn. She turns it over and over.

"Want some help?"

She doesn't respond. I was late getting here so we're not in our usual groove.

"Ms. Arguello?"

"You can call me Nancy."

A lump forms in my throat. She's never said that to me before.

"Here." I move her satchel to the floor, take the skein, and thread my hands through it. She smiles and starts winding.

We still have a few more skeins to go when David comes in.

"Hi, Mel." He stands over us behind the sofa and says to Ms. Arguello, "I've seen you around but we haven't met. I'm David Li, Christina Li's grandson."

"I don't know a Christina Li," she says. "Is she moving in?"

"No," he says. "She's been—"

"Yes," I interrupt. "She's new. David, this is Ms. Arguello."

He takes a second to recover; then he says, "Are you starting another scarf? What did you do with the other one?"

Uh-oh.

"I...I'm about to begin a muffler. For my grandson. He got a job on one of those oil-drilling things out to sea in Alaska where it gets very cold. Yesterday I...finished a...long sweater for..." Her forehead wrinkles as she struggles to think. "For my niece..."

147

"Huh," David says. "It looked like a—"

"Knitting doesn't always look like how it'll end up," I say firmly. "Ms. Arguello doesn't normally knit scarves, because they're too easy and no one wears them much anymore."

"Yes," she says, her confusion changing to wonder.

"But her grandson asked for one specially."

"That's right," she says, happy again. "How did you know?"

I give her my bright smile. "Judith told me."

David looks like he's adopted Ms. Arguello's confusion. I can't tell if he's going to let this go.

"Maybe you should talk to Dr. Jordan," I say, kind of loud, and nod toward the door.

"Okay." He turns on his heel and leaves.

———

As soon as the sun is down, Ms. Arguello packs up her satchel and leaves the Sun Room for dinner. I stay to watch the dark orange band of clouds over the sea. It's been an hour since David left.

I don't feel social. I don't want to sing. I'm not hungry. I wouldn't mind talking with Dr. Jordan but don't know where he is and don't want to get up to find him.

If I'm honest, I want David to come back. I don't know why he would, though, when I sent him away. I don't even know if he's still here. I could text him....

He doesn't know about Ms. Arguello. There's so much he doesn't know. Thinking about all the things to explain, about this place and the residents, about me, while dancing around everything I *can't* explain…it's exhausting. Maybe he went home. Probably for the best all around—

"It's dark in here," David says.

I'm too lethargic to be startled. How did I not hear him come in?

"Looks like you're melting into the couch."

I smile. It probably looks feeble. Rather than try to fix it, I say, "Feels that way, too."

I want to apologize but the words won't come. I don't want to open a door to a chain of explanations I don't have the juice to deliver.

But I have to.

"Sorry about before."

"No, it's fine. I get it now. Piers—" He wrinkles his nose. "Ugh, no, I mean *Dr. Jordan*, he told me she can't make new long-term memories, plus a lot of medical reasons why."

"I have to introduce myself to her every day."

David walks around to the front of the sofa. "It's sad that she can't get to know you. Or anyone else she doesn't already know."

"It's only sad to us. When her grandson asked for a scarf, it made her so happy, and she's been living in that glow every day for five years. Happily Ever After is a myth because the real world doesn't work that way, but it will for her. She's really going to live Happily Ever After."

David looks out the window a moment, then back at me. "And her grandson has hundreds of scarves. Or a side business selling them on eBay."

"He died in a fire his third day on the rig. Judith gives them away to shelters around the Bay. If you see a homeless person wearing a long heavy scarf, it's probably one of hers."

David sits. I want to analyze the distance he chose—at least a foot away—but then he pivots to face me. He was leaving room for his leg and now his knee is an inch from my thigh.

"Does everyone here have stories like that?"

"Doesn't everyone everywhere?"

"What about Mr. Knight?"

"Mr. Terrance Knight was a Baptist minister who got fired for marrying two men. To each other, I mean."

David shakes his head. "Terrible. Why do you always say his whole name?"

"Judith introduced him as 'the Reverend Terrance Knight' and he said to me, 'Oh, no, it's *Mister* Terrance Knight now and forevermore!' And so it is."

We sit quietly, just looking at each other. If anyone came in right now it would look weird, yet with the two of us alone, it's not weird at all. Even with how conflicted I am about everything, it feels comfortable. Warm.

"What about your boss, Judith? She seems as old as the residents in here except she's the warden. What's her story?"

"I can't give you *all* the answers. You need to figure some things out on your own."

"Uh-huh. So you don't know."

I smile. "Damn, you caught me."

He cocks his head. "Have I?"

His meaning is clear. I don't know what the answer is. I just know what it should be.

There's so much he can't know. I need to somehow become friends with him like I am with Holly and Declan, in small, light bursts...except keeping things from David feels like I've swallowed river stones that lie heavy in my stomach. It would feel too rotten all the time, being sort of close but not really. And I think I like him too much to burden him with a girlfriend like me.

"Is that hard to answer honestly?" he says.

I swallow. "You hardly know me."

"Everything I know so far, I like."

"Not my singing."

"I like it."

"That makes no sense."

"Makes perfect sense to me. I might only know one percent about you, but I like that whole first percent. Most people I meet don't come close."

I don't know what to say. I'm still trying to figure out how he could like my singing.

"When we met," he says, "I yelled and told you to leave. Remember what you did?"

"I left."

"Okay, do you remember what you *didn't* do?"

"Um..."

"You didn't tell me to go to hell. You didn't try to explain. You didn't even frown. I thought back later, remembering the look on your face.... You weren't bothered at all. I was pissed at you for helping my grandmother, and your face was still saying, *I'm sorry this is happening to you.*"

"I was."

He laughs. "I remember, that first moment, you reached out your hand toward us."

I smile.

"What?" he asks.

"I thought your hair looked like a Halloween cat."

"You..." He peers at me. "You were going to *pet* me?"

"No! I mean... that was in my head, I guess, but I wasn't really going to."

He thinks a moment. Then he combs his fingers through his hair to make it stick up. He leans toward me and tips his head down.

I reach out slowly and pass my hand across the tops of the spikes. He closes his eyes.

I'm free to look around: at his sharp cheekbones, his dark eyebrows, his lips. I run my hand through his hair, deeper now, fingertips on his scalp. I smile. I don't think this is what they mean by *heavy petting.*

He shows no impatience but I stop after a few strokes. I don't want him to think... except it *is* what I'm thinking. It's just not something that can happen.

He opens his eyes and leans back. "Does this mean you like me too?"

I laugh.

"What?"

"I don't know," I say. "Do people talk like this? About whether they like each other?"

"We can stop if you want to."

I nod. "Yeah, I like you. The whole one percent."

"Not the part that yelled at you."

"Especially that part. You were protecting her."

His hair's still sticking up. I reach out and smooth it down, watching his reaction to make sure it's okay. A voice in my head tells me to stop but I can't seem to obey it.

When I finish, David says, "No, most people don't talk like this. Most people are boring."

"Is that number five on your list of why you like me? I'm not boring?"

"No. It—"

"Wait, I *am* boring?"

"No." He laughs. "You're way too moody to be boring."

And there it is. I feel my face wincing and I force it to become a frown. Maybe I won't have to keep him at arm's length. He's figuring it out on his own.

"Sorry I'm moody—"

"Don't be," he says. "It's why I think I'm seeing the real you, not some show like people put on, trying to look cool or above it all."

"Huh?"

"It means I can see you're down right now, but you're the same person you were last night when you were happy. And even though you're down, you're helping Ms. Arguello, and you're smiling, and somehow it's not fake."

I rest my head against the sofa. "I don't know, David. Sounds like bullshit to me. If I'm smiling and it's not fake, how can you tell I'm down?"

"I'm very good at reading faces. Especially eyes."

"Is that so?"

"Yeah. It's my superpower."

I laugh. "What?"

He grins. "Dr. Jordan told me your theory. My super-power is I can tell when people are being fake."

"Oh really? Did Dr. Jordan tell you mine?"

"No. He said something about doctor-patient confidentiality. But I think I know what it is anyway."

"Please," I say. "I'm all ears."

He leans against the back of the sofa. "When I first came in here I could tell you were down but glad to see me. Then I started upsetting Ms. Arguello. To save her from feeling upset *now*—even though in a couple hours she'd forget it ever happened—you told me to leave. And you were *nice* about it."

"You didn't know about her memory."

David laughs.

"What?" I say. When he doesn't answer right away, I say, "Tell me."

"When you're happy," he says, "you're the light in the room. And when you're sad, you're still the light in the room. Most moody people take it out on everyone, dragging them down or snapping and being bitchy, but not you. I don't think there's a single bitch-bone in your body."

I swallow.

"That's your superpower," he says. "You're an uncommonly good person."

His face is close and getting closer. I want to glance down

at his lips but I can't look away from his eyes. He's going to kiss me, and I'm going to let him, but I shouldn't, but I want to, I really want to, and I see out of the corner of my eye the back of the sofa moving and David's staying still and *oh my God it's me—I'm the one leaning in!*

I blink and pull back. I exhale and turn to face the window.

"That was close!" David laughs. "Remember, not till our first date."

My face is heating up. I'm pretty sure he's covering. He was making no signs of stopping us. It's up to me.

"I'll have to remember that line for later...." David is saying. "What was it? I said you're a good person? That's all it took?"

"*Uncommonly* good," I say, like bantering is my autopilot. "That's the important part. I'm good, but I'm also *not common*."

He laughs.

I don't. I think about all the people who know I'm not as good a person as he thinks. Not just Zumi, either. The number of people who know what I'm really like could fill a movie theater.

"David," I say. It feels weird that I can't bring myself to look at him. I stare out the window at the dark. "You don't know me as well as you think."

"Good. I'd hate to think I already knew everything."

"It's not that. It's more like..." I close my eyes and take a breath. "I've hurt people before. And...I sort of can't help it. I don't think this is—"

"Now, *here's* a mood I haven't seen yet." He leans out from the sofa to get closer to my line of sight. "Is this the Great and

Powerful Mel, deciding the fates of all? You won't get rid of me that easily."

"I don't want to get rid of you. I just think we shouldn't—"

"Then we won't. Until we do. But don't worry, I can take care of myself—"

The lights flick on. I sit up straight and spin.

"There you are," Judith says. She's by the entrance to the hallway, hand still on the light switch, smiling.

"Sorry!" I jump up. "I'm coming right out."

"Good. You were late today so you're mine for another hour. And there's half a lounge act out here asking about you."

NINETEEN

Hamster is ACTIVE

Hummingbird is HOVERING

Hammerhead is THRASHING*

Hanniganimal is DOWN

I'm being punished.

Not directly, or on purpose, just...cosmically, or karmically, and a bit comically. After some singing, and then dinner, Mr. Terrance Knight calls me to the piano again and brings out the hymnbooks.

David sits on the far side of the room with Ms. Li and Dr. Jordan. I'm more self-conscious than usual but I don't know if it's having David here, singing songs I don't know, or my down mood. As Mr. Terrance Knight leafs through his hymnal for another song, I'm wondering what's a good way to say I want to lie down instead? My shift is done; I'm staying over because the room seems like it needs more magic. Yet if I'm singing to bring everyone up, but Mr. Terrance Knight has us singing to bring *me* up, and neither is working—

157

My phone rings. Strange, but I'll take it.

"Sorry, this is probably my mom or dad. They're the only ones who call." I walk toward the hallway and dig out my phone.

It's Connor. He's never called me before. Just texts.

"Connor?"

"You busy?"

His voice is tense, not his usual casual. It sounds like he's outside but I can't identify the background noise.

"Where are you?"

"With Zumi. Can you come?"

"Now? Did she ask for me?"

"No, but she knows I'm calling you."

David catches me watching him. We didn't really finish our conversation earlier and I wonder if he might be waiting for me to get off work, not just hanging around generally.

Sorry, David.

"Where?"

"On the beach," Connor says. "South Point."

I hear Zumi yell, "Bring more vodka!"

"What?!"

Everyone in the room looks at me. I walk quickly into the hall.

"You guys are drinking?"

"We're having a wake!" Zumi shouts. "For Annie! Price of admission, one bottle!"

I say, "This sounds like a bad idea."

"It's not," Connor says. "You'll see."

"I'll get there as soon as I can."

I hang up. It's too much ground to cover on foot—I need a ride.

I walk over to David. "Something's come up. Can you drop me somewhere?"

"Sure." He kisses Ms. Li on the cheek. "Gotta go."

"Don't hurry back. You kids have fun."

"See you tomorrow," he says.

"I have to change," I say. "Meet you out front in a few minutes."

In the bathroom I call HJ. I hope she can hear her phone ring. . . .

"Mel? Something wrong?"

Wow, I was right. It's really loud where she is.

"No, I'm fine. I'm with friends."

"What! Can't hear you!"

"Hang on!"

How can I have this conversation if I need to yell? I turn the sink faucet on full blast, sit against the wall farthest from the door, put my sweatshirt over my head, and hold the mic up to my mouth.

"I'm out with friends." I wince. "And I need a bottle of vodka."

"Mel!" HJ cackles. I can tell she pulls the phone away from her face briefly while she laughs. "And you think *beer* is gross!"

"Can you get a bottle at the bar and meet me out front in a few minutes?"

"How do you know where I am?"

159

"It's Saturday night. Will you?"

"Pats would *kill* me if she found out!"

"You said I should be a teenager before it's too late."

"Yeah, but hiding it from the grown-ups is part of the experience!"

"Next time I will, I promise. I'm just in a hurry and can't explain. Will you?"

She doesn't answer. The line isn't quiet, though. It sounds like human static on full blast.

"All right. One time only! Call when you're out front!"

"Thanks! See you soon."

————

When David and I get in his car, I say, "Sorry I have to go."

"It's okay. Where to?"

"The Rockin' Pony. You know where it is?"

"Just up the road. Why there?"

"It's those friends I told you about the other day, the ones having a hard time."

"They have fake IDs?"

"No, they're on the beach. I need to pick up something from my aunt first."

I don't say more. He'll see soon enough. I'll deal with it then.

"It's okay," he says after a moment. "You don't have to get into it. I don't mean to pry."

I reflexively want to tell him it's okay for him to pry... except it isn't.

Part of having him drive me was to finish our conversation, but the momentum's broken and I don't know how to start it up again. We drive in silence.

When David pulls up at the curb, I phone HJ. She answers and shouts, "I'm coming!" which triggers laughter from others in the background as she hangs up.

The door opens and lets out a blast of bar noise. HJ emerges in her sky-highs: stilettos so tall it's like she doesn't have feet. An unusual choice for a woman who's six feet tall barefoot, but HJ revels in her unusualness. She approaches the car carrying a ... long gray gym sock?

She squats by the passenger window and hands me the sock. Now I see it holds a bottle like a sleeve.

"You know, Mel, there's no takeout here. You're supposed to drink on the premises. It's illegal to take anything out. The cops I'm drinking with said so."

"You told them?"

"Don't worry, they're cool. Did you think that's my sock?"

"How much is it?"

"A fifth."

"A fifth of what?"

David says, "That's the size of the bottle."

"No, I mean how much do I owe you?"

"Nothing. It's a gift. For your sixteenth birthday."

"I turn seventeen in a couple weeks."

"And what did I get you for your last birthday?"

A very wet, sloppy kiss on the cheek, hard enough that it needed scrubbing later to wash the lipstick off.

"No, really, I want to pay you back."

"Can't. Slater—the bartender—gave it to me free. I'm good for business." She turns to face David. "Who's this?"

"My friend David." Then I say to him, "This is my aunt Joan."

"Call me HJ." She rests her forearms along the window frame. "So you're one of Mel's *friends*?"

"Pleasure to meet you," David says.

"Yeah. So, Mel, is this *the* friend? You know..." She back-hands my shoulder lightly.

"We're leaving now."

She nods at David. "You are, aren't you?"

He looks at her with a straight face... then he waggles his eyebrows.

HJ laughs so hard she reels back and has to grab the car to keep from falling.

The door to the bar opens. A guy in a blue button-down shirt and jeans steps out.

"Come on, Joan! I hear Kenny Loggins coming!"

"Jesus, Tom, your age is showing! I'm not riding the highway with you!" To us she says, "I hate when the band drinks themselves off the stage and it turns into Jukebox Night."

It's the cop from the beach. He's got shoes on but I can't see if he's wearing both socks.

"Duty calls," she says. "Don't make me regret this."

"Shouldn't you tell *me* that? Don't do anything *I'll* regret?"

"Be like me; I never regret anything!"

She stands up, raps the roof of the car, and strides back to the bar.

"That made no sense," David says.

"Yeah," I say. "We call her Hurricane Joan for a reason. HJ and regret have a complicated relationship."

"HJ. I get it. She knows what it means?"

"She's proud of it."

"So where next? Which beach?"

"South Point."

Again we don't talk as we drive over. I want to say the bottle's not for me, except maybe it is. I want to tell him we can't be more than part-time friends, but I remember Zumi calling me a martyr this afternoon for avoiding her last year. I could make up some reason, but I don't want to lie. This is the first time sitting with David in silence feels uncomfortable.

He parks in the lot but leaves the engine running. It's very dark out: only one lamp, no moon, out of sight of both the beach and the highway, with no one around.

"I'll wait here till you text me that you found your friends."

"Okay. Thanks for the ride."

"No problem."

I wait a moment. It feels bad to leave like this. I don't know what else I can do. It's too dark to see his expression.

"Okay." I open the door. "I'll text you."

As I walk across the parking lot to the path leading down to the beach, I type into my phone:

> I'm here. Thanks for the
> ride. And for waiting.

So I can just press Send when I get there and not type it while sitting with Zumi and Connor.

Next I text Mom. I have to tell her the truth since she knows my phone password and can pull up my location on a map anytime. She'd panic if she randomly saw me on the beach, thinking I might be alone. I tell her I'm here with friends—no other explanation—and I'll be back late. She tells me to be careful.

I see Zumi and Connor on a large beach blanket with a propane camping lantern. I press Send on my text to David.

The reply comes almost immediately.

> **Call me if you need a pickup or anything else. I can be back here in fifteen minutes.**

David must have pretyped it, too.

TWENTY

Hamster is *Running*

Hummingbird is *Hovering*

Hammerhead is *Thrashing**

Hanniganimal is *Down / Mixed*

Zumi sits cross-legged on a corner of the blanket, hard to see in her black hoodie. She trickles sand into a tall bottle. Connor sits to one side, facing the path, watching me approach. It's hard to tell in the dim light but he looks exhausted.

I say, "How long you been out here?"

"What's in the sock?" Zumi asks.

I dump out the bottle and say, "Admission is getting expensive." I try to hand it to Connor but Zumi takes it instead.

"I don't have bendy straws," I say. "And I don't see any cups. I guess if someone's sick, the vodka will kill the germs."

"This isn't just for me? You didn't bring any for you guys?"

I smile. It's definitely Zumi's kind of joke, though she said it seriously.

I don't want to drink at all. I wonder if I'll have to, if for no other reason than to reduce the amount she drinks. Maybe I could spill some. Drinking wasn't a thing with us last year and I want to know how much was in the bottle she's now filling with sand.

Zumi opens the vodka and holds it out to me.

"Make a toast."

"Uh…"

"To Annie's memory." She waggles the vodka. "From the heart."

I take the bottle and raise it a little.

"Um…to Annie." I think a moment. Then, "This town wasn't good enough for you."

Zumi barks laughter. It's real, raw, angry, and hurt, all at once. "*Damn*, Mel. You *nailed* it! I knew you would! Now drink!"

The instant before liquid touches my lips, I choke on burning fumes. Zumi rescues the bottle.

"God…" I can't stop coughing. "People…*pay*…to drink… *gasoline*?"

"Not much," Zumi says, examining the bottle by the light. "This is the cheap stuff. Now you, Connor."

He takes the bottle and holds it up.

"To Annie. We weren't good enough for you either."

Zumi nods, her face tight. Connor tips the bottle. I can't tell if he really drinks. He doesn't react anything like I did. Maybe he's used to it. He hands the bottle to Zumi.

She stands unsteadily. Connor and I scramble up to join her. She raises the bottle high, by the neck, but looks down, hidden by her hair. I glance at Connor. In the harsh light of the lantern, his face is tense.

After a moment, Zumi lifts her head and takes a long, hard swig. I see bubbles and no reaction. Apparently she's used to drinking gasoline.

"Annie!" she shouts over the crashing surf. "*Nothing* was good enough for you, *you fucking bitch*!"

She lurches forward—I grab on to keep her from falling, my adrenaline spiking as if the lantern below us were actually a fire. Connor takes the bottle.

Zumi leans on me, still facing the sea. "Fuck you, Annie! What a … goddamn … *waste of time!*"

I struggle to keep her steady.

"That's all you were! Selfish, shallow … waste of … of …" She drops her arms. "To hell with you …"

I pull Zumi off balance to get us to sit. We go down hard but it's okay. I wrap my arms around her and she hides her face against my shoulder. She's not crying but her muscles are clenched and I think her nose is bruising my neck.

She growls, "If you ever … ever … *ever* say 'I told you so,' I'll bite you."

I stroke her hair.

"I mean it. It'll leave a scar."

Connor sits and closes his eyes. He exhales like he's letting out air he's been holding a very long time. He wipes his face and opens his eyes. I reach out to him.

He tries to hand me the bottle. I roll my eyes. He sets it down and takes my hand long enough to squeeze it.

"You, too, Connor," Zumi mumbles. "Not one word. Ever."

I can't say I'm used to drinking gasoline already, but after a couple hours of tiny sips, I've discovered it's possible. Is this how it starts? My first steps along the path of Hurricane Joan?

Nobody makes me drink, but Zumi seeing us take turns keeps her talking. She needs to say these things and get it all out. Then I can go back to never drinking again.

"My uncle Leo," she says. "I don't think you ever met him."

I shake my head.

"He and Aunt Chris were happy for as long as I could remember. Then suddenly last year he moves in with us, gets a divorce, sells their house, finds an apartment, because Aunt Chris cheated on him."

She drinks and hands the bottle to me.

"He thought it was this one mistake. He'd been busy with work and said he blamed himself. Then he found out she'd been seeing this guy for two years, a few times a week. And there'd been other guys before that."

I pass the bottle to Connor.

"He said the betrayal was bad, but worse was thinking back over the years. About how when she came home from the mall, she'd really been with another guy all afternoon. Or her going out to pick up pizza, coming home with a smile and a kiss, saying it took an extra half hour because their order got lost."

Zumi reaches for the bottle, but Connor tips it up like he's drinking. She drops her hand.

"He said it was like being on some twisted reality show or

something, where he found out his wife was just an actor who had this whole other secret life…except that was her real life because those other guys knew the whole truth. *His* was her pretend life, so he couldn't fix it. You can't fix a relationship you never really had."

She's quiet a moment.

"But the worst—" Her voice catches. It's not grief I hear, or anger. More like disgust.

"He said the worst part was how much of the story he wrote himself. The errands she'd run nights and weekends— she didn't say why she went by herself. He assumed she was being nice since he worked hard all week. So yeah, she lied, but he filled in the gaps. He'd invented the lie he was living just as much as she did."

Zumi takes the bottle from Connor. She drinks and sets it between her crossed legs. Then she hits her forehead with the heel of her hand. Twice. Three times.

I push her hand away. "Do you know why your uncle filled in the gaps?"

"He's a sucker."

"He just assumed the best. Because he loved her."

Zumi takes another drink. This time she coughs.

"He's still a sucker."

"He wasn't," I say. "And neither are you."

"I feel like one. What's the difference?"

"You can stop feeling something if you're not. You can't stop if you really are."

"Uh…easy for you to say."

"I mean it. Who *you* are has *nothing* to do with who Annie was."

Zumi snorts. "She said it, all the time. I was her *muscle*. Connor was her *minion*. She didn't care about us. We were just the only ones willing to follow her around."

I want to soften this, but it's true. Zumi can only feel better once she talks it out and gets past it.

"Connor and I weren't with Annie," I say. "We were with you."

I reach for her hand but she pulls away.

"Don't," she whispers.

"Sorry—"

"I didn't get it till she packed her shit and jumped on a plane without saying good-bye. *You* didn't need to get hit with a sledgehammer to figure her out."

I reach for her again and she shrinks back.

"You just assumed the best with her," I say. "Because you loved her."

She looks down. "I loved all you guys."

"And we love you. Stop beating yourself up. *I* was the one breaking the rules when I asked you to take my side."

"Annie asked me, too, the day before you did."

"But you were in love with her. You can't ask a friend to choose you over someone they're in love with, even if you think that person's no good for them. That's the rule I broke. The heart wants what it wants."

If it surprises her I knew, or that I'm talking about it now, she doesn't show it.

Zumi shrugs. "She didn't love me."

"Did she say that?"

"Sneaking off to Paris said it. She *told* me she loved me, but like the *sister* she wished she had instead of Lulu. She talked about guys all the time...."

I catch Connor's eye. He presses his lips together and looks down.

Zumi sighs. "I just thought eventually...if she realized... that she might give us a chance...." She takes another drink. "God, it sounds so pathetic out loud! As if I could be so right for her that it would..." She laughs bitterly.

"It wasn't your fault," I say. "I saw how she was. She was leading you on, giving you little hints it might be possible."

"Why would she do that?"

"To keep her thumb on you. You know. If you kept thinking there might be a chance..."

Zumi slaps her hands over her eyes.

"God..."

She bends over, covering her face.

"Why didn't you tell me? No! Never mind. I wouldn't have listened. I didn't listen. God!"

"No, Zumi—"

"Yes, *Zumi*!" She sits back up. "I chased a straight girl for years, let her manipulate me, let her be mean to Connor! And I...I believed what she said about you!"

I get up...*whoa*...I'm really dizzy...and clumsily sit behind her to make a train. She tenses up, but when I hug her, she relaxes.

171

I wave Connor to sit closer. He slides over but not enough. I reach out and yank on his collar. He topples and spins and ends up with his head faceup on Zumi's lap. I'm sure he's going to leap away, but Zumi puts a hand on his forehead and he stays put.

"We want more than anything for some nice girl to fall in love with you," I say. "Until then, you'll just have to live with us loving you regular. Right, Connor?"

"Right," he says.

"Whoa!" I say. "He talks!"

"Only when I have to."

It's too dark to see clearly but I think Zumi's stroking Connor's hair.

She raises her head and turns. "How'd you know?"

I think about it. "It wasn't any one thing. It was just... obvious."

She looks down. "Was it obvious to you, too?"

"Yes," Connor says. "I knew in the seventh grade."

"Bullshit, Connor. Even I didn't know it then."

"You probably would have if you'd thought about it."

I say, "How come you never told Connor? I didn't think you had secrets from each other."

"It's not a secret," Zumi says. "I just didn't say it. I love broccoli on my nachos but I've probably never said that, either, or all kinds of other stuff you don't bother announcing to the world."

Connor says, "You don't have to say anything at all."

"Sometimes you should," she whispers. "We've been best

172

friends forever. Even when everyone thought it was weird, us playing in kindergarten, the screaming Japanese girl with the quiet ginger boy. I've never said I love you."

"You don't have to."

"I wanted to. I...I just didn't want you to get the wrong idea...."

Connor chuckles.

"But you *knew* what team I was on," she says. "All those years I could have been telling you, every time I thought it, and that's a lot."

"I never said it either."

"Hey, yeah. Why not?"

"I didn't want you to think I had the wrong idea."

After a quiet moment, Zumi combing Connor's hair, I move to stand. Zumi clamps down on my arms.

"Where do you think you're going?"

"My work here is done," I say.

"This is work? We aren't friends?"

"Yeah, but—"

"No buts! God, Mel!" She shoves Connor off her lap, twists around, and after flailing and yelps from all of us, she's lying on top of me. "Are we friends or not?"

"Yes."

"Cool. Can I kiss you? On the cheek, I mean. I don't want you to get the wrong idea. You're not my type."

"I know what your type is," I say. "And you don't have to ask."

"Neither do you."

She pecks me once. Then she hugs me fiercely, rolling back and forth, like brothers do.

"Connor," Zumi says, still hugging the breath out of me. "You want in on this?"

"I'm fine over here," he says. "It's weird enough now as it is."

TWENTY-ONE

Hamster is STUMBLING

Hummingbird is PERCHED

Hammerhead is THRASHING**

Hanniganimal is DOWN

Pain behind my eyes. Blinding. Throbbing. Can't think.

In bed. My bed. Hot. Sweaty. Trying to remember.

...*ow*...*ow*...*ow*...

Never felt pain like this. Not physically.

Flashes of memory...

Cold. Lying down. Connor facing the waves. Zumi behind him. Me behind her. Wrapped up tight. A burrito instead of a sandwich. Three pigs in a blanket. Zumi, Connor, and Mel. Dozing on the beach. How could I sleep? Blame the vodka.

Phone ringing. Zumi's. Waking. Tangled. Trying to answer. Laughing.

Talking. Shouting.

In back of Eddie's car. Pitching like a boat at sea. My head on someone's lap. Zumi and her brother whispering angrily.

On the toilet. Then next to it. Trying to clean up. Giving up.

DOO DE DOODLY DOO DE DOODLY—oh God *snooze SNOOZE STOP STOP STOP!*

Pills. Extra painkillers. *Not* the Ritalin.

Forgetting something...maybe a few things...

———

I wake up feeling sick again, the urgent kind. I scramble to the edge of the bed and see my trash can but don't remember putting it there. I recall it being full of papers, math scratch work, but there's no time to dump it out—I grab it and see it's empty and clean—not for long.

My stomach surges, like flicking a jump rope, and my body strains so hard I honk like a seal and can't stop.... There's a box of tissues here; I grab some, wipe my face, drop them in the can, and push myself back up on the bed, gasping like I just biked up a hill.

The door opens and Mom swaps my trash can for a clean one.

"S'okay," I mumble. "I'll just get it dirty again."

"You don't want that smell in here. I'm surprised you have anything left to throw up."

I vaguely remember puking before, more than once.

She puts her hand on my forehead. "You're not hot. Any other symptoms?"

I shake my head.

"What'd you eat last night?"

"Ravioli. At work. Same as everybody."

"Maybe it's just hitting you extra hard this month. Call me if you need anything."

A few minutes later I hear voices in the kitchen. They get louder. Strangely loud.

"What?!" Mom says.

I hear HJ's voice, too low to make out.

Mom yells, "Are you fucking kidding me?!"

More murmurs. Defensive.

"Have you *completely* lost your mind?! She's *sixteen*!"

The bed rolls beneath me. I squeeze my eyes shut.

"No! *No!* How could you?! You know how many meds she's on! What it took to balance her out!"

Fast murmurs now.

"*Alcohol* is a drug! God knows what it's doing, mixing with her other meds!"

My eyes hurt. Scratchy. Like they're trying to cry except I'm too dehydrated.

"She *wants* them! You know how lucky that is?! It's her chance to not turn into you! To not end up like Nolan!"

Somewhere my eyes find water and out it comes. Extra salty, burning like acid.

Footsteps pound down the hall. HJ's door opens. Closes. Opens again.

"No! Get *all the way* out! Get out of this house!"

I sink into my comforter as deep as I can go. Crying now, not just hot tears.

"No! Shut up! STOP TALKING! Get out!"

Shuffling now, not much, no voices.

"Christ!" Mom yells. The door slams. "Fine! Stay in there! Keep this closed! Don't let me *see* you! Don't let me *hear* you! Or I'll have your cop friends come *drag* you out!"

Mom walks back to outside my door. I try to stop crying so she won't hear. This hurts my head much worse.

She comes in and sits on my bed. I only feel it—my eyes are clenched and I'm burrowing.

"I'm sorry, baby. Sorry you heard that."

I try to say "It wasn't her fault" but I'm crying and muffled.

She strokes the comforter, trying to find me.

I open one eye. It hurts. Out through my comforter tunnel is Mom's knee, blurry, her hand on it, in a fist.

I try again. "Not her fault."

"She's the grown-up. Sort of."

"I'd have gotten it somewhere else."

"Why? You said you were with Zumi and Connor? Was it them?"

"They didn't make me. It was...just this once. I can't explain it...."

She rubs my shoulder through the thick comforter.

"You don't have to, as long as you promise not to do it again."

"I promise."

"We've talked about how alcohol and your meds don't mix and we don't know what might happen. I never harped on it since you didn't seem like you even wanted to drink."

178

"I don't. It was…it was just this one thing. I won't do it again."

"How do you feel?"

"Shitty."

She laughs gently. "Goes with the territory. But I mean, in your head. Your animals?"

"Down…but…not mixed."

"You were already down yesterday, with your period. Maybe this will be over soon. Chalk it up to another life experience."

"One time only," I croak.

"You know the best way to keep that promise?" She leans down and whispers, "Never forget how you feel right now."

"Ugh."

"Your prescriptions are ready. I was going to get them but it can wait."

"I'll be fine. I have nothing to throw up."

"I guess if I go now I can pick up something to help your stomach."

"Yes, please."

"I'll hurry back."

She kisses my head and leaves.

Through the pain I visualize her in time with sounds I hear: putting on shoes, messing with her bag, grabbing keys, then out the front door.

A minute later HJ's door creaks open. Then mine. Something bumps the bed.

I open my eyes. Aunt Joan is kneeling, hands clasped like she's praying. Her mascara is smeared, her face blotchier than usual.

"I'm sorry!"

"Why'd you tell her?"

"She thought you were sick! She was going to take you to a doctor for antibiotics!"

Aunt Joan drops her forehead down on her knuckles. "I shouldn't have done it. I don't know what I was thinking!"

"It might not look like it," I say, "but I wouldn't trade last night for anything."

"No!" She chokes up. "Listen to your mom. Don't be like me. Take all the meds in the world if you have to, just don't be like me—"

"I *want* to be like you—"

"No you don't! Don't ever say that!"

"Not *all* of you. Just the awesome parts."

She sobs.

I lift the comforter. She climbs in and I wrap us up tight.

Twenty minutes later Mom opens the door and sees Aunt Joan sleeping with me. I put a finger to my lips. Mom's face scrunches up and she puts a hand over her mouth.

She holds up a bottle of something with a little plastic cup on top. I shake my head. It throbs and makes me dizzy.

She nods and quietly closes the door.

———

My head hurts but isn't pounding now. I managed to eat a few dry pieces of toast around noon, not long after HJ woke and slunk into the bathroom for a while and then out the front door. Moving too fast makes me dizzy, so I'm parked on the sofa, but even sitting motionless I have tremors.

I text Judith after lunch that I'm sick. Then I text David to tell him thanks again for the ride. Also how I'm not well enough to come to the Silver Sands today. He texts back to drink lots of water and he'll talk to me later.

Declan texts me midafternoon. I totally forgot about our Chem lab reports due today. I tell him I'm sick but from something I ate so it's not contagious. He offers to do it all himself at his house, but I have some of the data here, and as tempted as I am, I can't let him do all our work. He'd probably do a better job without me, but...God, I can't think straight.

Not long after, Declan shows up with Holly. She drove him over and says she'll hang out and do homework she got assigned for the break. We deflect Mom's offers of snacks and drinks and more throw pillows and whether the room's too hot or too cold. "It's all fine, Mom."

She finally accepts this and leaves to do the weekly grocery shopping.

I hand Declan my lab notebook. That plus leaning over my laptop on the coffee table long enough to search for my other data files, and then e-mailing them five feet over to him, it exhausts me. I lie sideways and curl up on a pillow, my head next to where Holly works in a binder on her lap. Declan sits on the floor on the far side of the coffee table.

"Something you ate, huh?" he says. "Anything bad coming out the bottom end?"

"Declan," Holly says. I'm not sure if she's protecting me or just grossed out.

"Top only," I say.

"I don't think it's something you ate."

"You're a doctor now?" Holly says. "Or are you browsing BeYourOwnQuack.com?"

"It doesn't take a doctor to recognize when someone's sick from something they *drank*."

I don't say anything. I don't break eye contact with him, either. He holds it.

"Was it the King of Beers, or something more bottom shelf?"

"Vodka. From a bottle."

He laughs.

"You're hungover?" Holly says.

"If I say yes, will you think less of me?"

Declan says, "Not if it was really straight vodka shots...?"

I nod carefully.

He laughs again. "I had no idea you were a heavyweight."

"First time drinking anything."

"Even more impressive; skipping over Beginner *and* Intermediate straight to Expert. Well done. What was the occasion?"

"I'll tell you later," I say. "I don't feel well."

"You don't look well," Declan says.

Someone pounds on the door.

Holly says, "I'll get it."

She goes and opens the door.

"Where is she?" Zumi's voice is deep and unreadable, like it carries too many emotions to separate out. Probably because she drank way more than I did.

Declan points to me warily.

Zumi comes around the sofa, Connor right behind her. He looks lost but on alert somehow. He had a lot to drink, too.

"Hi," I say. "What's—"

"That yours?" Zumi points at my open laptop.

"Yeah—"

She sits hard on the sofa, knocking my knees. I stretch my legs out to give her room. She jams a thumb drive into the USB port and copies a file to the desktop.

"You, Declan," Zumi says. "You can't see from over there. This is too good to miss."

He comes around to stand by Holly.

I look up at Connor behind the sofa. "You know what this is?"

"No. She just called and asked for a ride."

Zumi says, "All last week I kept calling Annie, texting and e-mailing. Last night I finally got an answer."

I push myself up. "What'd she say?"

"Ten words." Zumi counts them on her fingers: *"Stop bugging me. Get over it. Maybe this will help."* She jerks the stick from the laptop and taps on the keyboard to open a movie file. "Sixty seconds of video can say a lot."

The screen shows Annie's room, pretty much exactly as I remember. The image shakes from someone adjusting the camera. It centers on Annie's bed with her rose-colored comforter. The view stops jiggling but no one appears or talks for maybe thirty seconds.

"What took so long?" Annie's voice finally says.

Then some soft talking. It's impossible to make it out. It might not even be speech, just mumbling or something similar.

Annie appears, backing up toward the bed. She wears her favorite white button-down sleeveless shirt, only with the top few buttons undone. Her arm is stretched out of frame. She briefly makes eye contact with the camera and smiles. Her head turns to reveal a bright orange California poppy over one ear—

I lunge for the laptop—but Zumi grabs both my wrists and drags me back to the sofa.

There it is. On the screen. Annie has pulled me up on the bed. We're kissing, clumsily groping each other's chests. It's messy, awkward fumbling, but not tentative, and not one-sided. It's enthusiastic, and not the first time, or the last. I had no idea she'd recorded anything.

Holly slams the laptop shut and grabs one of Zumi's arms. "Let go!"

Connor jumps over the sofa and they both pry Zumi off me. She glares at Connor hard enough to melt lead but he forces himself between us anyway.

I curl into a ball and wrap my arms over my head and Zumi leans around Connor and growls through her teeth, *"Don't…ever…talk…to me…again!"*

"Zumi!" Connor shouts in her face.

"What the hell, Connor?!" She pushes him back—he stumbles against the coffee table.

He stands up straight again and says to her, "We're going."

"Goddamn right, we're going!"

I say, "Zumi—"

"Fuck you, Mel!" she yells down at me. "Fuck you, *too*!"

I'm going to throw up. I scramble past Holly—my heel lands hard on her toes and she cries out—and push past Declan and run down the hall.

In my room, door closed, puking bile and bits of toast into the trash can, I'm convulsing way more than my body needs just to empty my stomach.

During the heaving and sobbing, the yelling stops and the front door slams. Holly and Declan talk through my door, asking if I'm okay and to let them in until I shout "Go away!" enough times that they finally leave.

TWENTY-TWO

Hamster is SPRINTING

Hummingbird is PERCHED

Hammerhead is THRASHING***

Hanniganimal is CRASHING / MIXED

Mom tries not to stare at me in Dr. Oswald's waiting room but she hasn't turned the page in her magazine for six and a half minutes judging by the analog clock over her shoulder but I'm not fooled because she never reads architecture magazines at home—it's just something to hold while we sit here trapped in silence since Dr. Oswald doesn't play any music out here though that's a small mercy if you ask me because there's nothing worse than psychiatrists I've had who play music in their waiting rooms that were really depressing ballads even if they use the karaoke versions without the lyrics because you still know the songs and usually the music is sad all by itself or just as bad they play happy tunes that don't match your mood and it makes you want to stand up and rip the damn speakers off the wall—

186

The door opens and Dr. Oswald says, "Oh, hello, Ms. Hannigan."

"Hello, Dr. Oswald. Mel's been having a bad couple of days. She's on spring break this week and she's been in bed. She didn't have the energy to bike over here—"

"I have energy only it's just on the inside which is really a better place for it since when I let it out I just start crying and can't stop and after a while it hurts even to breathe—"

"Her period started on Saturday and it seems unusually bad—"

"I'm right here you know and I can talk about my own bodily functions—"

"She went out drinking with friends Saturday night and spent Sunday vomiting—we've had a talk about that—so alcohol might be part of this."

Dr. Oswald says to me, "Did you throw up your medication yesterday?"

"Oh!" Mom says.

"I don't remember much of anything yesterday but I know I've only skipped one day and that was today so I must have taken them Sunday but probably before I threw up—"

"Wait," Mom says. "You didn't take your meds this morning?"

"I turned my alarm off yesterday and forgot so it didn't go off today and I slept in really late and then I didn't think about it till afternoon and by then it was too late even though I know I'm supposed to take them anyway if it's more than twelve hours till my next dose but I've been doing okay lately so I didn't want to double up—"

"Mel, you *haven't* been doing okay!" Mom turns to Dr. Oswald. "She's been hiding in bed, crying off and on, ever since I got home from shopping yesterday."

"I've just been stressed out and sad and anxious but for normal reasons with stuff that's going on with my friends and at school and work and not my screwed-up brain making up stuff that's not real—"

"Mel? Mel?" Dr. Oswald is saying my name over and over again like a parrot.

"What?"

"Two days without meds isn't the end of the world, but you need to get back on. It's also possibly contributing to your nausea and dizziness. I see you're having tremors, too."

I hold up a hand and it's shaking and I let it fall again.

"You should definitely take your meds as soon as you get home. We need to get you back on schedule. Let me check my notes, but I think you should take some lorazepam now. I have a bottle in my desk."

She glances at Mom and they both nod so I nod too so we're all nodding.

"But can't we talk out here because I'm really worn out and don't want to move at all and I didn't even want to come since I'm so tired and we could just talk next week but Mom wanted me to get out of the house like I don't get enough vitamin D or something—"

"Come on, Mel," Mom says and pulls me up out of the chair and walks me into the office while wiping my nose and face with some tissue.

Mom sits me on the sofa and I lie down and slide a throw pillow under my head but then she pulls me back up while Dr. Oswald hands me a couple of tablets and a coffee mug filled with water or just filled halfway actually and I think it should be funny because of how I only fill up cups halfway at work so residents won't spill so it's like I'm one of Dr. Oswald's residents but it's not funny because it just isn't and I can't really imagine anything being funny now when all I want to do is lie down again so I do.

Dr. Oswald walks Mom to the door and closes it and then walks back to her chair—

"Mel? There's a tissue box by your head on the end table."

I feel more tears on my face and think it's weird she saw them before I felt them but I don't want to reach for the tissue box so I just wipe my face and nose on my sleeve and sniffle—

"You might feel better if you sit up. Just like how facial expressions can affect your mood, so can posture and body mechanics."

I don't care if she's right or not—there's no way I'm moving when all I want to do is—

"You didn't bring your charts?"

"No I didn't even want to come today but Mom made me but I can tell you all about the whole Hanniganimal zoo if you want or I could draw it from memory but I really don't feel like it since I don't even want to sit up and I just—"

"...Mel? Mel? I need you to hear something."

"I can hear you just fine Dr. Oswald since I'm—"

"The combination of menstrual hormones and alcohol

can definitely push you off balance. The interruption of your medications would exacerbate this, but it's only been a couple days and I don't think that's enough to explain how you're obviously feeling."

"I'm not super off balance right now—I think maybe I didn't just have a hangover but I'm also coming down with a cold or something because I'm tired and kind of cranky which is really unusual—"

"Mel, you're crying. Do you know you're crying?"

I wipe my face and sniffle and say "I'm just really worn out and—"

"Mel, I think you're under some emotional stress that's adding to everything else. Has something happened? You look like a deer caught in headlights."

I feel that way a lot of the time but I'm usually much better about not showing it—

"If something hurts, telling me won't make it worse or make it more real. It's already real. Telling me what you're thinking can only make it better. And you can tell me *anything* here. I promise, *nothing* bad will *ever* happen because of what you say in this room. Only good things."

I find that really hard to believe—

"Can you tell me what's wrong?"

I don't want to...but maybe I should...because I don't understand....

And I need to now because my superpower is failing...I can't stop the memories from playing in my mind again and again...when I could block it all out I didn't need to understand but now I do because I can't make it stop....

I don't want to say the words...but now I have to....

Except I can't...I'm crying too hard...and my hands are blocking my mouth...trying to keep myself together... because my face hurts so much it feels like it's cracking apart and falling into pieces....

————

I can't look at Dr. Oswald while I talk—it's hard enough to let myself hear what I'm saying—but I can't figure this out and how else can I explain it to Zumi if *I* don't even understand it? I'm thankful the pills I took a half hour ago slowed my Hamster down to subsonic speeds so I can think and speak more clearly, but it's not enough.

"So you became intimate with Annie?"

"We kissed a lot, and...touched each other."

"Did it feel good? Did it feel normal?"

"I...I don't know how to explain it. It's all too complicated. Everything's tangled up with everything else."

"Did you tell anyone?"

"No!"

"Not even your doctor?"

"Argh! I didn't have a doctor!" I cover my face with both hands.

"This happened before your diagnosis?"

"Yes, right before!" I take a few breaths. "We moved here the summer before freshman year and I was really depressed...."

"Right after your parents divorced, which was after your brother—"

191

"It's got nothing to do with that! I was just in a new town and school. Then in the first week of high school I met Annie, Zumi, and Connor. This stuff I'm talking about now was a year later, when we were sophomores."

"Okay."

"I was starting to feel better and my family was glad I was getting my energy back. We all started having more fun with me up and running again. Zumi loved it and we became even better friends. Annie didn't like it so much."

"She was jealous of you and Zumi getting closer? But you said Annie didn't love Zumi back."

"It was all about Annie keeping Zumi on a leash or tied up in the front yard but never allowed in the house. But she didn't want Zumi or any of us to leave her. I think Annie got worried that Zumi and Connor might start following me instead of her."

"How did all this turn into you and Annie starting to—"

"That's what I'm asking *you*! I didn't even like Annie by then! But Zumi goes to her grandmother's for Thanksgiving and suddenly Annie's all over me, and I'm on her, and I turn into this whole different person—for a whole week! Then it's like I woke up and became myself again, and I have no clue who had been at the controls. I ended it and we got in this huge fight over what an awful manipulative asshole she was. The next day I'm in the psych ward."

"You were having your onset and this stressor made it bloom into a manic episode."

"*And* it made me a lesbian for a week and then switched it back off again."

"So you believe you're heterosexual?"

"I don't have to *believe* it. I just know."

"I'm sorry, that was poor phrasing. I mean, if you don't feel attracted to girls, was this an experiment? Why were you—"

"I don't know! I'm telling you all this because I need *you* to tell *me* what it was! I've never looked at a girl except that one time. If I was attracted to girls I'd want Zumi—she was my best friend *and* I love her *and* she's beautiful, but I've never wanted to *kiss* her, not like Annie and I were kissing. Not like I want to kiss David."

"Who's David?"

"He's...this guy...I was on a...I mean, we haven't... That's a whole different thing. The point is, I *want* to kiss *him* and *not* Zumi or any other girl. But the bipolar made me a lesbian for a while and that's scary."

"Bisexual. Your encounter didn't switch off your interest in guys. And bipolar disorder causes hypersexuality, especially during manic episodes, and it affects thoughts and emotions in many challenging ways, but it only magnifies your feelings. It doesn't change your preferences."

"So I'm bisexual and afraid to admit it?"

"Not afraid, necessarily. Possibly not aware."

"How can I not be *aware* of my own preference! You're saying I'm hiding it from myself? That could apply to everybody!"

"Bisexual doesn't mean equal attractions. You could be on the edge of the spectrum where you might not think about it. Like you're eighty percent into boys and only twenty percent into girls, so you don't notice the less intense impulses compared to the strong ones. Then a manic episode magnifies everything, enough to boost a feeling of *I want to spend time with that pretty girl* into the more intense feeling of *I want to kiss that pretty girl.*"

"Great, so manic episodes don't *make* me bisexual, they just make me realize I already am even though I don't feel that way the rest of the time? That's practically the same thing."

Dr. Oswald nods. "I can see how it would seem that way. Does it upset you? To discover that you can love girls, too?"

I think a moment.

"No," I say. "I just hate that I did it with *Annie.*"

"You mean instead of Zumi?"

"What? No. I know what I said before, but I didn't feel that way for Zumi even during that week I was with Annie. I guess she's not my type? I don't know, I haven't thought about that yet in the two minutes since I found out about this!"

"So it's just about Annie? You'd be just as upset if Annie were a guy you didn't like who your friend had a crush on?"

"Yes! But...it's even worse than that. Zumi was in love with Annie and thought Annie didn't love her back because she *couldn't,* but now she's found out *two* of her friends, who she thought were straight, were *both* bisexual *and* keeping it secret from her *and* getting together behind her back! So I *feel* like I've *always* felt—like scum of the earth for hooking up with the one person my best friend always wanted, even though I didn't actually want her, only now she knows and hates me for it. And to top it all off, you're telling me this wasn't the bipolar's fault!"

I wipe tears from my face.

"Bipolar disorder doesn't change your preference," Dr. Oswald says. "But going from zero to intimate with someone you didn't like, knowing it would hurt your best friend to discover it, you can totally blame it for that."

"Plenty of girls do that sort of thing without being bipolar."

"Is that the kind of person you are?"

"Hell if I know. Depends on the day. On the *hour*. I can be all kinds of different people."

"You said you stopped being friends with Annie and tried to get Zumi to side with you?"

"Yeah. I was kidding myself. I knew she'd never leave Annie."

"And you never told her what happened?"

"If Zumi found out, it would have crushed her. The best thing I could do was disappear. What she didn't know couldn't hurt her."

Dr. Oswald doesn't say anything. I glance over.

"*That's* the kind of person you are, Mel."

I look back up at the ceiling. "Doesn't matter. It's over now. I couldn't protect her from Annie *or* me."

"She's devastated because she knows the real Annie now. Maybe it's time for her to know the real Mel?"

I laugh bitterly. "Right! *Oh, Mel, you're bipolar? Thanks for telling me! That explains everything. We can be friends now. I've always wanted a ... BBF—a Bipolar Best Friend!*"

"You're not bipolar, Mel. You have a bipolar disorder. You also have vibrant blue eyes, a wonderful personality, a tendency to undervalue yourself, and many, many other things. None of those things *are* you."

"What am I, then?"

"A person who changes and grows all the time. What do you really think Zumi would say if you told her everything?"

"Probably the same thing she said about Annie on Saturday. That she doesn't know who I am anymore. That she never did. How she can't be friends with someone she doesn't know."

"Would she be right?"

"Yes! That's why I don't want anyone to find out!"

"But if they don't know you, are they truly your friends?"

I fold my arms over my face. "I really, *really* can't talk about this anymore. Please. I want to go home."

"I'm not telling you to reveal your condition to anyone. That's for you to decide. But you seem to crave true intimacy and that's not possible with you keeping so many secrets. Not just about your past, but about who you are."

I shoot her a look. "Do *you* tell all your friends everything about you?"

"Of course not. But... there will always be a severe limit to how close you can feel to anyone when you don't even let them know your real name."

I quickly look away. Tears are coming back. I fight it. I don't want to be crying when I go back out to Mom in the waiting room.

"It's just a name. It's not me."

"If it didn't matter, you wouldn't be afraid of it."

"Is our time up?" I can't see the clock from here.

"Yes. Take your meds as soon as you get home. And please think about what I said."

"What, about the alleged importance of real names?"

"About what it will take to get the relationships you want. Eventually you'll have to give someone a chance."

"A chance?"

I think back to Dr. Jordan telling me to give Dr. Oswald a chance. I wipe my eyes again and look at her.

"A chance to know and love the real you."

TWENTY-THREE

Hamster is *SPRINTING*

Hummingbird is *FLYING*

Hammerhead is *THRASHING*****

Hanniganimal is *CRASHING / MIXED*

Dr. Oswald told me the pills she gave me would wear off and I should take more to be able to sleep but I didn't want to sleep because I had a plan so even though Mom watched me take my other meds when we got home she hadn't heard what Dr. Oswald said so she didn't say anything when I didn't take any Ativan.

It took all night to compose an e-mail explaining everything starting with the divorce though nothing about Nolan since that's not part of this at all plus Holly and Declan don't know about him but everything else after that like my depression and the move and coming out of it the following summer and then ramping up sophomore year and growing manic and the whole episode with Annie and our blowup and then my onset and hospitalization and diagnosis and the chaotic year trying to balance my meds in as much detail as I could remember.

It felt bizarre at first to explain everything I've been trying to hide for so long but once I got going it all came flooding out like a dam broke inside of me even though I still don't want anyone to know but with that video it's way worse for them not to know what caused it so I have this terrible thing to explain and the only way to make them understand is to tell them I'm not guilty by reason of insanity.

The final explanation is only a couple dozen pages long but I deleted and rewrote a lot more than that through the night trying to get it all right and not confusing which was hard because of how tangled up all this stuff is and how any one thing doesn't make sense without all the other things so how could I explain it all when the beginning makes no sense without the ending though maybe I should at least break it up into paragraphs or something but I don't know how to since everything is connected with everything else.

My clock says it's 6:08 a.m. which means my alarm is going to ring in seven minutes but I'm wide awake and I'm not going to take my meds yet since I was very late yesterday so I'm going to take them earlier than that today but later than usual to try and split the difference and get back on schedule by tomorrow so I turn off the alarm and think maybe I should set a new one for noon to take them then but no I'll remember and maybe when the time comes depending on how I feel I might want to take them a bit later than noon.

I get up and go to the bathroom and make some noise on purpose so Mom will hear me and won't think I'm skipping my meds again today.

"Mel?" She's waiting for me in her robe at my door. "Take your meds?"

I nod and try to look sleepy from having just woken up to not have to explain anything since she'll just worry I'll forget to take my meds later or argue that it's not a good idea if it didn't come from Dr. Oswald and it works since Mom smiles and tucks my hair behind my ears and heads for the shower and I think that my eyes being puffy from crying off and on all night long probably helped sell it.

I don't want anyone who saw the video to think I'm not telling everyone else so I send my explanation out as a group e-mail to all four of them and because I want them all to read it as soon as possible to minimize the amount of time they hate me I also send them a group text telling them to check their e-mail when they wake up.

I see the progress bar for sending my message stretch across the screen and I think about how after a couple texts and unanswered calls from Holly and one from Declan on Sunday asking if I'm okay it all stopped and I've heard nothing from anybody since and I think they must be embarrassed for themselves or for me or both and probably just want it all to go away or for *me* to go away—

The text won't send—it's stalled—*shit!*—I remember now that when Holly started calling my phone Sunday I didn't want to talk to anyone and I switched it to Airplane Mode to stop getting hammered by it all but still be able to use my alarm.

I switch it back and more texts from Holly appear that are all variations of *Are you okay?* and *Call me!* from Sunday.

mostly and a couple yesterday but nothing from anyone else so maybe nobody wants to hear my long explanation for that video clip from over a year ago and maybe when they get it they'll roll their eyes and all my explanations will just be annoying and pitiful—

Swoosh! My e-mail and text both go out so it's too late to call any of it back now.

I don't want to sit still but there's nowhere to go and Mom will just worry and ask me questions if I don't stay in bed and it seems like a long time with no replies to my text but I look at the clock and it's been less than two minutes and I doubt anyone is even awake yet and won't be for a while since there's no school this week—

Mom pops her head in to check on me and I manage a smile and then she leaves for work so now I can get up but I still need to be quiet since Aunt Joan doesn't go to work for another hour though she's pretty much been hiding in her room—

My phone buzzes with a text from Zumi.

> **Stop sending me your**
> **pathetic rants! I'm**
> **blocking you!**

She did a Reply All and no more texts appear but if they did I wouldn't be able to read them since everything's blurry with my eyes flooding and now water is smeared on the screen and I smash a pillow over my face so Aunt Joan won't hear me cry but I can't stop and it's getting worse and I have to get out of here!

I can't take my bike because Aunt Joan would definitely

hear that so I keep sobbing into the pillow and sneak out the patio door and out the side gate and now I can get away and she won't know I'm gone since she never checks on me before leaving in the mornings.

The sun's not up but it's getting light and the only thing I can think to do is go to the track and sit on the bleachers but I remember it's spring break so no one's going to be there jumping and why does watching people running and jump-ing make me feel better anyway when I never actually saw Nolan do it even one time but it doesn't matter since it won't work now when it's just a sandbox if no one's jumping in it but thinking about it that way tells me how to fix this.

I need to get to school faster but I'm still pushing the pil-low against my mouth and nose to muffle my crying though I don't need to be as quiet out here and it's awkward to hurry while holding my pillow up with both hands but there's no way I'm going to go back home so I drop it on a neighbor's lawn and take off running.

———

Long jumps are a lot harder than they look even knowing what you're supposed to do like concentrate on how fast you run more than how hard you jump because the coaches say how far you jump is mostly about how fast you're running when your feet leave the runway and then it's about controlling your rotation and keeping your balance in the air and not so much about actually jumping like a kangaroo.

There's a middle-aged woman wearing gray sweats jogging here but I ignore her and keep jumping again and again while trying to run as fast as I can and also plant my right foot on the board but not past it without slowing down or screwing up my strides so I can jump as far as I can without falling backward when I hit the sand—

"Excuse me, hello?" the jogger says while stepping in front of me waving a hand and looking at me but with her head kind of lowered down like she's ducking under a low tree branch or something and she says, "Do you need help?"

I shake my head and pace away from the pit and turn around to make another run at the board but now she's standing in front of me blocking me with both hands up and she says, "What's wrong, sweetie? Can you tell me why you're crying?"

I try to say "I'm not crying" but it's hard from gasping so much with all this exercise and I think maybe she's confused by me breathing hard and the sweat running down my face and I wave her out of the way so I can make my run—

"Okay," she says like she doesn't believe me and then she says, "Is there someone I can call for you? You really shouldn't be doing this without shoes. Look, you're bleeding."

I look down and see the tops of two of my toes are scratched and a little bloody from the jumps but it doesn't hurt or anything and now that I'm looking down I see a few red splotches along the runway and I wonder when I took off my shoes and socks but now that I think about it I don't remember putting them on this morning and I see I'm still wearing my sweatpants and my zombie teddy bears sleep shirt too—

"Let's call your mom or dad," the jogger says and starts

walking sideways toward the bleachers while she keeps watching me and she says, "Is this your phone on the bench here? Let's call someone and get you home."

I run by her and she flinches as I pass and I scoop up my phone and run up the bleacher steps—

"Sweetie, wait!" she calls.

I yell "It's okay I'm going home now!" and I keep on running and glance back once to see her watching me and shading her eyes but she isn't following me.

I'm not really going home but I can't stay here with this woman in the way and it wasn't working anyway and I think it's because I can't really imagine Nolan here since he was never actually here and there's only one place I can think of that I can get to where I've seen him and been with him and that's where I need to go and now that I think about it the last time I felt like this I rode up to that happy place and it helped me feel better so that settles it except the Golden Gate Bridge is over twenty miles north but I can get there in maybe a few hours—

My phone buzzes and I see it's a text from Connor.

You okay?

I don't want to answer but I also don't want anyone to get worried since then they'll come looking for me so I answer him:

Yes.

Zumi shouldn't have said that. I'll talk to her.

I remember now the e-mail I sent this morning telling them stuff but I can't remember the details but I do remember Zumi is really upset with me and has every right to be—

He texts again:

I'm coming over.

No! I stop walking and text him back:

Don't.

Coming anyway.

Not home.

He doesn't reply and I try again:

Don't come.

He doesn't answer—*shit!*—and I'm too far to get back before he gets there not that I'd go anyway—

I get a text but from Declan this time:

Zumi's a bitch.

I answer:

No I was a shitty friend.

He doesn't reply right away and I start walking again and then he texts:

**A friend of my cousin
has bipolar disorder and**

205

that dude is truly a shitty
friend. If you've had it all
this time and we had no
idea, you're a hero.

Holly calls and I decline it and then she texts me:

Mel?

I text her:

Can't talk.

Declan says he's texting
you. I've been so worried!
Want me to come over?

No.

Are you sure?

Busy.

I'm glad you told us. You
can't even tell. Declan and
I knew you got weirdly
excited sometimes and
other times were in the
dumps but are you sure
you're not just really
moody?

Yes.

Don't be embarrassed
about that video! No big
deal. We've all done stuff
we'd hate for anyone else
to see. I didn't like her but

I can't deny she was good
looking! And don't even
think about Izumi. They
deserved each other.

My eyes are flooding again.

Got to go.

You sure you're okay?

Fine.

Okay but call me later
anytime. Day or night. I
mean it! ANY TIME!

I push the phone into my pocket and it buzzes again but I'm
dizzy and shaking and can't think straight and I really need to
be away from everything and everybody and more importantly
they need to be away from me but I can't let them figure out
where I am or where I'm going or they'll try to stop me so I give
in and look at my phone and see it was a text from Connor.

I see your bike through the
window. I'm going to keep
knocking till you answer.

No!

My phone rings and it's Aunt Joan and God knows what
Connor just told her so I better answer and convince her
everything is fine but first I clear my throat so it won't sound
like I'm crying.

"Hi," I say.

"Where are you, Mel?"

"Walking."

"At seven thirty? On vacation? You *always* take your bike. You never just go for a *walk*. What're you really doing?"

"Just walking—"

"Mel, you're crying! You sound like you're gargling snot! Your friend Connor here says you're having a fight or something? Not with him but with someone else?"

"It's fine. I'm just...walking."

"Mel, where are you, *exactly*?"

"By...the firehouse..." My hands are shaking so much I can barely hold the phone to my ear and I feel like I'm being hit by a tall wave at the beach and getting knocked over and I really have to get off the phone!

"I'm fine...please Aunt Joan...don't call Mom—"

"Why would I call your mom?! Is there a reason I should? Mel? Mel?!"

"No! Please...I...I can't talk! Just let me walk...there's something I have to do...*please don't call Mom*! I'm just *walking*!" Only I'm not walking anymore and I'm turned all around—

"Stay by the firehouse. I'm coming to get you—"

"No! I'm *fine*!"

Shrill beeps in the background tell me she's started her car without the seat belt on.

"Mel, I'll be there in ten minutes. Stay—"

I turn my phone off so they can't track me and then I turn north and start running.

TWENTY-FOUR

Hamster is *Running*

Hummingbird is *Speeding*

Hammerhead is *Thrashing*****

Hanniganimal is *Crashing / Mixed*

I've lost track of time but it's been hours since I left the house. I still have plenty of energy but I'm built for biking, not running, so jogging stabs a knife into my side. My feet stopped bleeding not long after I left the track. They hurt a little but not too bad, except I caught sight of them once and it wasn't pretty so I'm avoiding looking again. The clouds are low and thin—I can see there's blue sky above them but I'm mostly surrounded by gray fog—and my superpower is gone. My life keeps flashing before my eyes and I'd give anything to stop it.

A few blocks ago I turned off the Great Highway and next is getting through the Presidio to reach the bridge but I can't remember the way. There are so many loops and dead ends, I'll never get there without a map.

I need to use my GPS. Mom's probably frantically driving

around, on the phone with HJ, maybe Dad by now. Did Connor go back home or is he out looking for me, too? I saw all the worrying about Nolan enough to know what this looks like, and now I can't stop thinking about it. Whatever worrying is going on back home, I have to try and stop it.

I switch on my phone and see it's just past one in the afternoon. The screen lights up repeatedly: missed calls, voice mails, from everybody, including Dad. I can't bring myself to read or listen to any of it. I just need to text Mom that I'm all right and get directions through the Presidio and switch it off again—

It rings and I drop it—I scramble to pick it up and see that it's Mom. How did she know to call right this minute? Has she been calling over and over for hours? I don't want to answer or hear her voice but I can't ignore it.

"Mom, I—"

"Why are you up by Lands End?! How'd you get up there?"

That's how she knew—I popped up on the phone tracker.

"I walked. I'm fine. I need—"

"You're *not fine*, Mel! You just walked twenty miles! And you're crying! Can you hear yourself? Take some Ativan! Did you bring any?"

"No, I…" I didn't bring any meds. I was going to take them at noon—I guess I can't now—

"Stay right there! We're coming to get you!"

"I don't want to see anyone—"

"You can do that at home!"

"It's okay, Mom, I need—"

"Dad and I are getting in the car right now to—"

I hang up.

I check the map. Left on Thirtieth, right on El Camino, turns into Lincoln, three miles to the bridge.

Mom calls again and I decline it.

I see more replies on the group text I sent this morning. They're all from Zumi.

> **I'm sorry Mel.**
>
> **I hadn't read your email when I texted you.**
>
> **Connor came over and made me read it. He was furious. I've never seen him like that before.**
>
> **Call me?**
>
> **I'm so sorry.**
>
> **Please come home.**
>
> **At least tell me you're okay.**
>
> **Please?**

That's all, and a good thing, too—everything's getting blurry and hard to read. I look for voice mails. A few from Mom and HJ, one from Dad, and two from Zumi. I tap on Zumi's.

"Mel, I'm sorry. I didn't mean what I said. Call me, okay? Call me."

Her voice is completely flat. I've more than broken her heart—I've stomped it into pulp. I wipe my nose and face on my sleeve but it's hopeless so I give up and tap her next message.

"Mel...I don't understand...." Zumi's voice is trembling so much I barely recognize it. "I've been so horrible and blamed you for everything. Why do you still want to be my friend?"

She coughs away from the phone a few times.

"I don't know," she whispers, so softly I can barely hear her. "But I really need you. Please tell me you're okay. And come home."

I drop the phone again. I'm sobbing so hard it's like I'm convulsing. I can't stand what I'm doing to them being out here making them worry but the only way I can pull myself together again is to get to our spot—Nolan's and mine.

I text Mom:

> There's something I need
> to do. Can't explain now.
> Please don't worry.

She calls again and I decline again. I need to switch the phone off but I fumble and it's hard with everything so blurry and my hands shaking so much—

A new text appears. I wipe my eyes and see it's from Mom.

> You need help, Mel. Deep
> down you know this. Let
> us come pick you up so we
> can get you the help you
> need. Please, Mel, leave
> your phone on so we can
> find you.

A cold flush runs through my body. I *do* know what she's saying, and I'll do *anything* not to go back in there. I switch off the phone.

Now it's a race.

———

It's the end of April, freshman year, on a Saturday. I'm in Zumi's backyard tree house with Zumi, Connor, sleeping bags, popcorn, and videos on Eddie's laptop. Annie said her mom wouldn't let her stay over but I saw the look on her face when the idea came up. I was glad because it would be cramped enough with just the three of us and Annie never let us talk about anything important. Maybe she'd have made an exception today since they buried Zumi's grandfather this morning, but I think Annie's not being here means she doesn't want to deal with it, that or the idea of being outside in the damp cold all night, or maybe both.

Eddie's laptop runs out of battery by ten and we don't want to run down the flashlights, so the only light now comes from the back porch through the large window opening of the tree house.

After some quiet sitting in the dark, Zumi asks softly, "You think about your dad much?"

"Sometimes," Connor says. "I barely remember what he looked like."

"You think he's in heaven?"

"Maybe. I don't know where that is, though."

I smile.

"I don't believe in heaven anymore," Zumi says. "People keep

telling me how when you die you get to be with everyone you love, but it doesn't add up. Your mom loved your dad, but then he died, so if she falls in love with someone else and gets married again, when they all die and go to heaven, who would your mom be with up there?"

"Both of them?" I say.

Zumi leans over and swats me. "Maybe a threesome's not everyone's idea of heaven!" She sits back again and sighs. "Everyone can't get what they want if they want different things. What if... what if you want to be with someone, but they don't want to be with you?"

"Maybe heaven isn't about getting everything you want," Connor says. "Maybe it's about not wanting anything anymore and being happy about it."

"That makes no sense," Zumi says.

"It's Buddhism. You should know—"

"Because I'm Asian?!" She leans over to whack him but can't reach and she falls across my outstretched legs.

"No, because we spent two weeks on it in sixth grade, remember? If you don't want things, you won't be unhappy about things you don't have, and you won't be worried about losing things you do have."

"Yes, professor," she says, still sprawled out. "But I love pizza. If I die and go to heaven, and instead of getting delicious pizza all the time, I just stop wanting pizza, that'd be hell."

"If hell has pizza," I say, "it's probably nice and hot."

"There's no pizza—that's what makes it hell." Zumi rolls over and lies faceup, head on my thigh. "Either nothing comes after, or it's nothing good, or it's nothing like we want it to be."

"Nothing is the best answer," I say. "Sleeping is good. Sleeping in is better. Sleeping forever can't be that bad."

My eyes are getting itchy and wet. I better do something. . . .

I twirl some of Zumi's hair around my finger. "Sit up."

She does and squeezes between my knees, her back to me. I can't see but I don't need to. I braid her hair tightly because I know I can't tie it off and it'll just slacken, but that's pretty, when it's braided but loose. I take my time. Zumi's hair feels good sliding between my fingers.

"You've never had anyone die, have you, Mel?" Zumi whispers.

I don't trust my voice and just keep braiding her hair.

"I hope you never do. Take it from Connor and me. It really sucks."

TWENTY-FIVE

Hamster is *RUNNING*

Hummingbird is *FLYING*

Hammerhead is *THRASHING*****

Hanniganimal is *CRASHING / MIXED*

The Golden Gate Bridge is often encased in fog or low clouds but not today. It's all burned off now. The sky around the deep orange span is cloudless and the kind of bright blue no crayon can deliver. It's so beautiful it crushes me. It hurts my eyes and my wheezing chest.

Nolan and I broke a lot of rules the day we came here together: no switching buddies, no climbing on anything, no leaving the group, and others, too. Every third grader had a sixth-grade buddy for the field trip, and of course they wouldn't assign Nolan to me—they won't put siblings together—but once we got off the bus we secretly switched buddies and then us Hannigans ducked away to break the biggest rule of all.

It was so pointless, eating bag lunches at the café below the south end of the bridge for half an hour without getting to go

216

on it. The teachers said the field trip was to visit the Exploratorium, not the bridge, and eating lunch there was only a treat while we were nearby. Supposedly we didn't have enough time and walking on it was too much to deal with given our numbers and chaperone ratios. But that's what made it easy for Nolan and me to slip away and scramble up the stairs, sticking to the west sidewalk, out of sight of the lower tourist areas. We wanted to walk all the way across but we completely misjudged the distance. We only made it as far as the south tower.

Today, as I walk toward the pedestrian entry, there are two cop cars parked here at an angle. Two women in uniform stand together, drinking coffee. They're not going to let a crying girl walk onto the bridge. I force myself to cough, and keep coughing, as I pass them. They have no problem letting someone with the flu on the bridge and they're happy to turn away and keep their distance.

When I'm far enough to stop coughing, I do, and the crying doesn't resume. My whole body aches. It was more like a seizure than just crying, my screwed-up brain off the rails. It's a huge relief to stop. All around me the sky is bright, the air crisp, and there's enough wind to kick up the whitecaps far below me. It's spring break lots of places so the bridge is busy.

After a few minutes of trying to walk calmly and not start running again, I reach the south tower. I drop to my hands where Nolan and I sat together and scramble around till I find it. Scratched in the concrete, by the curb at the base of the tower, are faint letters less than half an inch high, so no one would notice and remove them.

I sit down, cross my legs, lean back against the tower, and look out over the Pacific, listening to rumbling cars pass behind me. I put my hand on the initials, to feel them, to protect them, and to shield them from the curious eyes of people walking by and looking down at the crying girl sitting on the bridge. Hot tears run down my face but the sobbing doesn't start again. I bask in what I came for, an oasis of desperately needed peace. I can feel my heart slowing down.

I love HJ and she's the closest anyone comes to being like Nolan and me, but she doesn't get it as much as she thinks. Mom gets it less and Dad doesn't get it at all. Nolan was just like me, or I'm just like he was, and sometimes I can't bear how much I miss him. He was the only one who would have completely understood.

Something occurs to me. I can't believe it never has before. I take out my phone, turn it on, and take a picture of Nolan's scratches. Now I'll still have it if the city ever repaves this sidewalk. As I move my finger to quickly switch the phone back off, I see Zumi sent me an e-mail, a reply to the big one I sent this morning.

> I'm sorry Mel. I can't even tell you how much. I don't know how.
>
> Connor has been pissed at me for only two days and it's unbearable. It makes me think how you must have felt except I was pissed at you for over a year. God I'm sorry.

I hope you never have to hear Connor shout at you. Sunday after we left your house he yelled at me all the way back to my place and it was awful. I hadn't told anyone I liked Annie. I hadn't even come out. I can't blame you for hooking up with her when I never said anything. Especially when she was the one who came on to you and you didn't even want to, but just sort of had this thing happen to you.

And me not figuring it out wasn't even what made Connor so angry. I didn't want to admit it was my fault so I tried to argue. I said I mostly hated how you went behind my back and kept it a secret. That's when he really blew up.

He said something like "Mel could have thrown Annie under the bus to stay friends with us, but she knew it would hurt you too much to find out Annie DID like girls but just not YOU, that she was NEVER going to love YOU!"

I said I'd rather have known the truth but he just got angrier because you DID try to tell me back then and I ran you out of my house!

The last thing he said was "If you can't see how big a sacrifice she made for you then fuck, Zumi, I don't know, I really don't know." Then he drove away and wouldn't answer my calls for two days. It was terrible. The next time I saw him was this morning when he showed up at my house and made me read your email about everything and how hard it's been for you.

Typing all this is making me sick. God I feel horrible. I'm so sorry. Please let me make it up to you. You're a better friend than Annie ever was and I don't want to lose you again.

Please?

I drop the phone in my lap.

Seeing Zumi this upset after being exposed to the real me for less than a day, how can I stay friends with her? I hate drama and now with *everything* out in the open, it can't be avoided. It was my fault, letting people get too close—

"Are you okay?"

It's some guy in his thirties, on a bike. He wears multicolored Lycra shorts and a jersey.

I stand up. I don't want to alarm anyone. "I'm fine."

"You sure?"

"Yeah. I just...lost somebody."

He frowns. "I'm sorry. There's going to be netting under the bridge soon. I know it's too late for whomever you lost, but..."

I smile and walk back the way I came. I try to concentrate on what to do now. Mom and Dad are probably close and if they find me they're going to put me in a hospital. I need to hide someplace and figure out how to switch off the phone tracker so I can talk to them without them finding me until I can convince them to just let me come home.

Maybe I can call Connor to come get me. He's the only one I can think of who might be able to help but also stay a safe distance. And I can trust him . . . except . . . he didn't know the truth about me before. That changes everything. I remember from when Nolan would ramp up, how everyone seems to think it's okay to lie to people like us if it's for *our own good*. Now that Connor knows the truth, maybe I can't even trust him anymore—

My phone rings. It's David.

Perfect. He doesn't know what's going on.

I answer. "Hi, David."

"Hey, Mel. Sorry I've been out of touch. I busted my phone on Sunday. I got a new one today and I'm . . . ah . . . calling to see how your spring break is going."

"Where are you?"

"In the city. I'm just about to head home—"

"Can you pick me up? I'm at the Golden Gate Bridge."

"Um, sure. How'd you get up here?"

"I'll tell you later. I'll be at the café in a few minutes. You know where that is? Below the—"

"I know it. I can be there in a couple minutes, maybe before you if you're not already there."

"Great, thanks."

I turn off my phone and start jogging.

In a few minutes, I trot down the stairs to the parking lot. David was right; he got here before me. I hop in his car.

"Nice shirt," he says. "Are those zombie teddy bears?"

"Yeah." I tuck my feet to the side so he can't see I'm barefoot.

"You okay?"

"Yeah."

"Take you home?"

"No! Can we...can we go to your house instead? I'd like to see it."

"Um, okay." He combs his fingers through the hair over his forehead, checks for traffic in the mirrors, and then puts the car in gear. We pull away from the curb.

I should use this time to explain what I've told all my other friends. Except I'm not up to it. I'll need to be a lot stronger than this to take seeing his face when he finds out the truth about what goes on in my head.

I fumble with the window controls but it won't open....

"Sorry, they're locked." He unlocks them.

I roll my window all the way down and lay my head out on the frame. We're on the highway heading south. I'm exhausted now but still buzzing everywhere: in my head, in my chest, in my arms and legs. I close my eyes and the fierce wind blows my face dry.

"Hang in there, Mel." David rubs my shoulder a couple times. "We'll be home soon."

———

We turn off the freeway. My eyes pop open and my heart jumps. I duck out of sight.

"What's wrong?"

"Nothing, I...it's fine. I just don't feel well. Where do you live exactly? You've never told me."

"Not far from your place. If you're sick, I should take you home—"

"No! No. Your house, okay?" He doesn't answer. "Okay?"

He runs his fingers through his hair again. "All right."

David takes a left turn and it pushes me into the car door.

After a moment, he says, "You're not carsick, are you? Can you tell me what's wrong?"

"No," I whisper.

"Whatever it is, you can tell me. It'll be all right. I promise."

"You can't promise that."

"I can. I am. Please tell me. What's wrong?"

He touches my hand and I shrink away.

"Are we there yet?"

He pulls over to the curb.

"I really like you, Mel."

He's using the wrong kind of voice. My alarms go off. I glance up at him.

"Remember that. Okay?"

Oh God no...

I pop my head up—we're in front of my house—Mom and Dad are trotting from the front door and across the lawn—

"What are you doing?!" I yell at David. I see a police car parked across the street and a uniformed officer jumps out of it. "Drive! Go! *Get me out of here!*"

David shuts off the car.

"*Please!* They're going to lock me up! I thought you liked me! You said—"

"I do like you—"

"Prove it! Get me out of here!"

223

He grabs the key but pulls it out.

"Help me, David!"

He lowers his head to the steering wheel and says "I am" but I can barely hear it—

I see my dad and I slam my hand on the door lock before he can open it—he reaches in and I slap his hands away—behind him on the porch Connor holds Zumi next to HJ whose hands cover her mouth and another cop in uniform beside her runs forward and he looks familiar but I don't know why—

Dad gets the door open and I scramble away and grab David's arm but Dad's got hold of my waist and he says "Mel you're safe come on out" and Mom cries and says "Please baby it's going to be okay" but it's *not going to be okay*!

"How could you do this to me?!" I yell at David. *"How could you! You're a liar! You lied to me!"*

"I'm sorry," he says with his head on the steering wheel and he still won't look at me. "Dr. Jordan said this was the only—"

"What?!" I scream. *"This was all a setup?!"*

I claw at the door frame but can't get a grip and Dad drags me out and I thrash and flail—

"Don't touch me—get away from me—let me go—"

It works and I'm free and I push off the ground and run but after three steps a huge weight hits me from behind and squashes me down on the grass and before I know what happened my arms are behind me and I'm pinned and can't move except for thrashing my legs below my knees but there's nothing to kick—

"Please baby they're not going to hurt you," Mom says but she's crying so maybe she doesn't believe it and just wants me to give up.

I'm lifted by the shoulders—it's HJ's friend Tom and another cop which is *bullshit* since they're not supposed to send uniforms to a 5150 and make a scene in front of your house and—I crane my neck to look back at the porch, at my family and friends united against me....

I see what's going on and go limp but the cops don't loosen their grip as they maneuver me into the back of the patrol car and shut the door.

This can't be happening. I must be hallucinating. How else to explain David's betrayal, and the patrol car that isn't supposed to be here, and how one of the cops hauling me away is the only cop I know, and Dad's holding Mom when they're divorced, and Connor's holding Zumi when they're not a couple and can never be a couple...

But mostly I think this can't be real because Zumi is sobbing on Connor's shoulder and there's *nothing on earth* that could make her cry like that.

TWENTY-SIX

Hamster is HIBERNATING

Hummingbird is ASLEEP

Hammerhead is THRASHING*****

Hanniganimal is CRASHED

I shouldn't have fought this.

Here I can stay curled up on this soft chair. They leave me alone. There's hardly anyone around. They don't let me stay in bed. This is close enough.

I don't have to do anything. I don't have to take care of myself. They give me a clean gown and slippers every morning. They change the gauze on my battered feet. They feed me. They tell me where to go. They give me my meds.

I can stay in this dreamy haze...like I've just woken up... barely awake...nothing to worry about...or think about... no reason to move...it's a dream come true.

I have nothing here. That's what I want. Nothing to do. Or worry about. Or think about. No one outside has to worry about me. I don't know why I fought this. This is the only place I get everything I want. Nothing.

I'm a different kind of mixed. Miserable and serene.

Heaven and hell are the same place.

———

It's chilly in here. Maybe there's a heater vent near some other chair . . . but I don't want to get up.

A skinny blond girl cries in the corner, her face on her knees, rocking. It's been hours. She's exhausted but keeps going. I know what that's like.

I want to tell her it's okay. They'll take care of everything. She doesn't have to worry. Or be worried about. I want to tell her . . . but I don't want to get up. Or talk. She'll figure it out.

"Mel?"

It's not time to eat. Not time for meds. Not time for bed. I'm not breaking any rules. Rules are things you *can't* do. I'm doing nothing.

"Mel, you have a visitor."

I shake my head. As little as possible. Without looking up. Maybe the less I move, the sooner she'll leave.

"You're not supposed to have visitors in your first twenty-four hours, but they're making an exception."

I don't move. I already shook my head.

The nurse squats by me. "The doctors said it could be here, in the big room. This almost never happens. They're letting him in since he's a retired psychiatrist. It's Dr. Jordan. He's a friend of yours? You should feel lucky."

She says this nicely. Not like I'm being ungrateful. Like she's happy they're doing me this favor. It's wasted. I don't want it.

"The doctors said he could come right in, but he doesn't want to unless you say it's okay. May he come in?"

I shake my head again.

"Are you sure? I think you should see him."

Another shake. Stronger. To end this.

The nurse sighs. "What do you want me to tell him?"

There's nothing to say.

She stands up. "Won't you tell me why?"

I close my eyes. She'll go away eventually.

"If I don't tell him something, he might think you didn't understand and come anyway."

I glance up. It's the older nurse with the short black hair. It's not glossy like Zumi's. It's dyed and looks like tar.

"Tell him—" I cough. I can barely understand myself. I'm hoarse. My lips and tongue feel thick. I try to clear my throat but don't have the energy. I just mumble through it.

"Tell him he's not my doctor."

———

The cafeteria is a counter and four tables. They don't make food here. They bring in stacks of premade trays to choose from. I think this room is only for the small wing where I'm staying. Short-term involuntary holds. Teens only. Not more than a dozen when full.

There are only two other girls now. We don't talk or look at each other.

The orderly is a Samoan guy with a buzz cut. He and the

tar-headed nurse guide us into the cafeteria. We line up at the counter. If you can call three girls a line. There are no trays yet. They tell us to sit down.

I find a seat facing a wall. The windows are too bright. I don't want to see outside anyway.

One of the other girls comes to my table. Just that much, her sitting in front of me, looking at me, not even talking... it tires me out.

"You don't recognize me?"

I haven't really looked at her. But trying not to will make this last longer.

She's my age. Curvy. Latina. Her wavy dark hair is slicked back. Probably just greasy from being here. Despite that, she's pretty. She seems familiar. Can't remember. Wearing identical hospital gowns, under these fluorescent lights, nobody looks normal.

"It's okay," she says. "I didn't recognize you either, till I saw... you know..." She waves vaguely. "The signs."

I guess she means my brown hair, blue eyes, and freckles. The signs of Mel Hannigan.

"I'm Sofia Martinez."

Her name's familiar... but... no... too foggy...

"Still nothing? I used to run with Gloria and Tina Fernandez?" She smiles. "*Now* you remember! Don't worry, I'm not with them anymore. Fucking psychos." She laughs. "I should talk, huh?"

Someone comes in the room carrying a stack of trays.

"What are you in for?" Sofia says.

229

I don't want to talk. Especially with any part of Team Fernandez. Even ex-members. But...I also want the easiest path.

I point at my temple and twirl my finger around.

"An actual lunatic, huh?" she says. "Good. Otherwise getting locked up would violate your human rights."

"You too?"

"No. My human rights are being violated." She leans back. "If I explain it all now, I won't have anything left to tell you at Group this afternoon. And since Lacey never talks, you'd be the only one talking. You want that?"

I shake my head.

"I figured. So what's up with Zumi and Connor?"

Huh? What does she care? And what makes her think I know? Maybe she heard about me getting between Zumi and Tina at school.

"I don't know," I say. "We're not friends anymore."

"Really." Sofia looks at the window at the light.

The nurse walks up to our table carrying two stacked trays in each hand:

"I bet you thought we'd only serve boring healthy food, but on Wednesdays we have treats to celebrate getting halfway through the week. You can choose healthy broccoli stir-fry..."

She sets down two trays. They have chopped green vegetables in the large compartment. The smaller compartments have cubed carrots, applesauce, and breadsticks. It's all covered in plastic with drops of water underneath.

"Or...you can have...this..."

She sets down the other trays. Under the wet plastic, instead of vegetables, is a corn dog.

I melt into tears.

———

The psychiatrist, name already forgotten, waits patiently. I think for me to answer a question. I don't remember. Or didn't hear. I want to be back in the big room. Not in his office. But I like him. He looks like he's from India and sounds like he's from Texas. I like how he speaks softly. And lets me sit curled up in this chair.

He says, "You understand you'll need to talk to me to be able to go home, right?"

I don't want to go home.

"You're clearer now than yesterday when you arrived. We had to sedate you but that wore off long ago. Your low energy now is natural—I mean it's not medication. You're back on your normal regimen, with different dosing to ease you back on track. It'll take time."

He pauses. Maybe to give me a turn. I pass.

"We spoke yesterday but you might not recall. Do you know why you're here?"

I twirl my finger around my left ear.

He smiles a little. "That doesn't actually mean anything, unless your purpose is just to offend people. What do you really mean?"

I don't have to answer. He knows what I mean.

After a moment, he asks, "Do you know what dysphoric mania is?"

"Just what it feels like."

"How's it feel?"

"Like...being excited and miserable at the same time."

"Yes. That's why your family admitted you. It's an extremely dangerous state of mind even if you say you don't want to hurt yourself. It's the same state your brother was in when—"

I curl up tightly and wrap my arms around my head.

"We don't have to talk about that now," he says. "I know you don't believe it, but you'll be able to move on and feel better once you talk it through and process it."

I don't want to move on. Or feel better. I only want to stop worrying people. And hurting them.

"I let you skip Group yesterday, but not today. I'll see you at four o'clock."

———

Dr. Dharni wants a volunteer to start. Sofia doesn't disappoint.

She asks me, "Did you try to kill yourself?"

I shake my head.

"Me neither. So here we are again, the Suicide Group, where the only girl who actually tried to kill herself..." She points at Lacey. "...is the one who won't talk."

Lacey is sandy blond, wispy, pale, and curled up on her chair like me. She stares at the floor.

232

Sofia says, "They think I tried to kill myself with pills just because I wasn't careful enough with how many and what I was mixing."

"I think it's fair to say," Dr. Dharni says, "that only people open to dying would be so careless with something so dangerous."

"I was trying not to care about anything at all. It usually works out fine. It's not the same thing as trying to kill myself. I sure as hell don't want to die. That wouldn't be any fun at all. Maybe I took the wrong mix because I'm stupid. Is that a crime, too?"

"Except you're very smart," Dr. Dharni says. "Anyone who listens to you for five minutes can tell since—"

Sofia snorts. "Who listens?"

"—your vocabulary gives you away."

"Got a great rack, too." She tips her head. "Guess which gets me further?"

Dr. Dharni doesn't want to guess.

Sofia says to me, "So you didn't want to die, either. Why'd everyone think you did?"

"I went to the Golden Gate Bridge—"

She laughs. "No wonder you're here! Did the cops pull you off the railing?"

"They didn't grab me till I got home later."

"Wait, you went to the Golden Gate Bridge, looked around, and then went home, like thousands of tourists? How come none of *them* are locked up in here, Dr. Dharni?"

He doesn't answer.

"How'd your friends find out you're here?"

How does she even know? Doesn't matter. "They were there at my house."

"You got an intervention? *I* woke up alone strapped to a hospital bed. I got moved here when they saw what they pumped out of my stomach."

I close my eyes.

"I guess that's why you're hiding, huh?" Sofia says.

"I'm not hiding," I say. "I'm...locked up."

"You still haven't said why. It's not for sightseeing on the bridge. You must have done something else."

I can see this is going to be harder, and last longer, if I keep trying to dodge. I take a deep breath. "I ran to the bridge—"

"From here? Okay, that's extreme, maybe, but not—"

"Barefoot. In my pajamas. After staying up all night."

Sofia apparently has no snappy comeback to this. I keep my eyes closed and have no desire to fill the silence.

After another moment, she says, "Why?"

I don't want to tell her about Nolan or the exact reason I chose that spot to run to, but I can say the part that's not a secret anymore.

"I have bipolar disorder. Yesterday I did a really crappy job of hiding it, so the secret's out. That's why I'm here. Because now everybody knows I'm someone to treat differently. To keep an eye on. Can't relax around. Can't be themselves with. High maintenance."

"Oh, so you think you're like the Down's syndrome kid now? The one people try to act normal around but can't quite pull it off? The kid they'll be nice to for a minute in the halls but don't really want at the good parties?"

I don't answer. I'm done.

A chair creaks and I hear footsteps. "Come over here," Sofia says, her voice now off to my right.

I open my eyes. Sofia's standing by a waist-high bookcase below the windows. I shrink in my chair and glance at Dr. Dharni.

"It's okay," he says.

I don't want to...but...the path of least resistance...

Most of the view through the bars is parking lot out front and to the left...with trees and grass and flower beds to the right, and...a picnic. A big blanket, some bags, and two people. Zumi is lying sprawled out next to Connor sitting cross-legged with his laptop.

"This place takes people from all over the county," Sofia says. "And we all look like drowned rats in here. I didn't realize who you were till I saw the signs."

Behind Connor stand two sandwich boards, the ones Zumi's dad puts on street corners to advertise apartments for rent. One holds a sign that says, "WE LOVE YOU MEL!" with hearts drawn around it. The other sign is solid white with *48* written on it in black marker.

Zumi jumps up, grabs something, and erases the *48*. They must be dry-erase boards. Then she leans back. Now the board reads *47*.

"Get it?" Sofia says. "Forty-seven hours left on your seventy-two-hour hold."

Zumi stands and stretches, arms straight over her head. She bends one way, then the other, and turns to face me—

I squat behind the bookcase.

"Okay," Sofia laughs. "*Now* you're hiding."

I sit down and push back against the books.

"I've seen other people out there, too. Maybe parents and grandparents? *I* get nothing. *You* have a welcome-home party on pause outside with a goddamn countdown."

Sofia walks back to her chair and plops into it.

"You seem so...*vanilla*. I thought everyone was making a big deal over nothing, but bipolar disorder? Now I get why your feet are all gauzed up. Maybe you really do belong in here. Either that or you're just another pathetic attention-seeking privileged white girl."

Some choice.

TWENTY-SEVEN

Hamster is *RUNNING*

Hummingbird is *FLYING*

Hammerhead is *SLOGGING*

Hanniganimal is *DOWN / MIXED*

Midday on Friday, they give me a canvas bag from Mom holding clean clothes. I take the gauze off my feet and check that the scabs are fine before I change out of the hospital gown and into my street clothes.

In the big room, Lacey is wedged in a corner. Sofia stands at the window. I walk up next to her and look out at the empty lawn.

"Zumi and Connor around front?" Sofia asks.

"I don't know where they are."

The whole truth is more shameful. I asked Mom to tell them to leave. I can't bear seeing anyone. I don't want to stay locked up, but I also don't want to leave this protected zone where it's okay to be broken since everyone else is, too.

Sofia shakes her head. "So you get to go home. I guess you

gave the doctors the right answers. Mine got me two more weeks. Who was that black woman? I've never seen her before."

"A doctor I know on the outside. She helped them decide to let me out."

"Jesus, how many doctors do you know?"

"You want me to recommend somebody?"

Sofia snorts.

"It's not fair, how you get to leave when you're the only one of us who actually belongs here. Lacey and me, we're just addicts."

"She's in withdrawal? How do you know? She doesn't go to our school and never talks."

"She buys from my uncle." Sofia glances at the clock. "Two minutes left. They do like following their rules. Good luck out there, *tontita*."

"What's that mean? Tina called me that last week."

"*Tonta* means *idiot*. But if you smile and say *tontita* it means *silly little girl*."

"I don't think she was smiling."

"Well, you *did* disappoint her. You know, when we first met."

I think back. "When you guys were chasing me away from tables in the cafeteria?"

"Testing you. Seeing if you'd stand up to us. But no, you kept running away, tail between your legs. Till Annie rescued you."

Before I can reply to this, Dr. Dharni calls, "Mel? Time to go."

"Remember," Sofia says. "We don't talk on the outside. At least not like this."

"You mean you won't come to my birthday party?"

She smiles and shakes her head like I'm a silly little girl, a *tontita*. "Not in this lifetime. But if you need something for it, I can hook you up. I know a guy."

Dr. Dharni shows me into a side room where reunions can be private. Mom and Dad jump up and smother me in hugs and kisses and apologies and I let them.

When I'm standing apart again, Dad says, "You sure you're ready? You can stay longer if you want to."

"I didn't want to come in the first place."

His face tightens and I quickly say, "I'm kidding. I'm sorry I lost it. But if I signed up for the fourteen-day plan, I probably wouldn't pass eleventh grade. Aren't you proud of me? I arranged to have my breakdown during spring break so it wouldn't ruin my life."

He hugs me again. "Doing what you need to do is always the best thing."

I clamp down hard on my emotions. I know a lot of why I got locked up was because I couldn't stop crying. Better not start again now.

Dad lets go. While everyone shakes hands with Dr. Dharni, thanking him, I see Dr. Jordan stand up from a chair across the room.

"Forgive me?" he asks.

"Do I have a choice?"

"You do. I promised your grandmother I'd do whatever

I could to help you. Being friends is a bonus. I hope I can do both, but keeping you safe will always come first. I'm sorry."

"I'm upset with David for tricking me, not with you for asking him to."

"It was quite a struggle. He really didn't want to lie. I'm afraid I used his feelings for you against him to change his mind."

He hugs me. He already knew about my broken brain so I don't have to worry he'll start treating me different. Besides, he's family now. The grandfather I never had.

Walking through reception, someone taps my shoulder. I turn and barely have time to see it's HJ before she stoops and wraps her arms around my waist and lifts me up in a hug much stronger than her bony frame seems capable of. I hug her back, our ears pressed together, my feet dangling.

She starts walking without letting go. She says, "You got dragged in here so you get to be carried out."

"Joan," Dad says. "Let the girl have some dignity."

I squeeze HJ tighter and she keeps carrying me. Mom and Dad follow a few steps behind. Dad shakes his head but he's smiling a little.

Dr. Jordan holds open the glass doors for HJ to carry me out. She sets me down and grabs my head with both hands and kisses me hard and long on my cheek.

"Happy early birthday, kiddo."

I can tell it'll take scrubbing to get the lipstick off my cheek again this year, but I'm going to leave it.

It's bright outside. I squint and turn to the parking lot to look for the car—Zumi's right there and almost tackles me except HJ catches us.

"I'm sorry, Mel!" Zumi whispers in my ear. "I couldn't just leave!"

I see Connor standing off to the side, looking uncomfortable.

"I love you, Mel," Zumi says. "You hear me? I love you."

I haven't hugged her back. I want to crawl away to my dark warm bedroom and hide.

"C'mon, Zumi," Connor says. "She just wants to go home."

I hug her back loosely. "I love you, too." It sounds like someone else is saying the words.

Connor puts a hand on Zumi's shoulder and gently pulls her away. I can't face her. I don't want to see the look in her eyes now that she knows what I am.

She shoves something into my hand. An envelope.

"Call me later?" Zumi says. Connor pulls her back some more. She lets him and says, "As soon as you … you know … as soon as you can. Okay? Promise me?"

I need to go home, into my room, before anyone figures out I'm not much better than seventy-two hours ago. I'm not as worked up or crying but I'm still mixed, and … there was something stabilizing about the quiet empty big room with its clean white walls … but outside, with all these people, talking, hugging … I'm ramping up again.

Only worse this time because now everyone's staring at me.

———

As soon as we get home I move my bike out to the garage. Dad asks what I'm doing and I say, "Putting it where it belongs." No one says anything to that, and I feel bad for saying it. Nobody knows the reason I ran to the bridge on foot was because I couldn't get my bike out of the house without being heard. I have no immediate plans on doing it again, but if I need to, I want my bike.

Mom makes me a grilled cheese though I'm not hungry. I quit halfway through and no one tries to make me finish it. Aunt Joan asks about the envelope Zumi gave me. I'd forgotten it was in my hand till I had to set it down to eat. It's blank and sealed. When I don't say anything she lets it drop.

I say I'm worn out and want to go lie down in my room. Everyone walks me there. Mom slides the trash can over to hold my door open. No one says anything about it. I'm fine with that.

After more hugs, Dad leaves. So does HJ. Back to work. It's Friday.

I don't want to open Zumi's envelope. I don't want it haunting me, either. I try to block it out but my superpower hasn't come back. Maybe it's gone for good.

Dear Mel,

My phone really did break and I didn't get a new one till Tuesday morning. Then Dr. Jordan told me you were on the run and something terrible could happen if we didn't get you back. Your mom gave us the password to track your phone so we could hit refresh over and over while she was out driving around looking for you. When you popped up near the Presidio, I jumped in my car to drive up while Dr. Jordan called your mom to tell her I was going to get you. He said you might be paranoid, and the only way to get you back would be to pretend I didn't know anything, and tell you I was taking you somewhere but drive you home instead so they could check you into a hospital.

I gave Zumi this note since you probably don't want to see me now, but I hope you don't want me to stay away for long. I hope you can forgive me.

Dr. Jordan said I did the right thing but it doesn't feel like it. He wasn't there. And I don't care what HE thinks. I care what YOU think. Now that you're home safe, are you glad I did it? I hope you can tell me at least that much because even if it was the right thing I still feel like the worst kind of asshole.

I think I know maybe five percent of you now and I still haven't seen anything I don't like. I didn't like how you were upset, but finding out you've been carrying all this around and able to keep it together, it makes me like you even more. I understand if you hate me now but I really hope you don't. Either way, I'm here for you.

David

My plan backfired. I thought reading this would let me forget about it but it's making me think more.

I text him:

I understand.

243

He answers right away:

But are you glad?

I think about what I want to say. It's not easy.
He texts again:

**Please tell me the truth.
Even if it's hard.**

I think with David the path of least resistance is the absolute truth.

You lied to me.

**I'm sorry. Dr. Jordan said
it was the only safe way to
get you home.**

But now I can't trust you
anymore. I'll always wonder
if you're doing it again.

**Dr. Jordan said you
weren't thinking straight.
He said if I told the truth,
we might lose you.**

I have to go.

**Tell me how to do it right
and I will.**

Do what right? How to act
around someone whose
brain doesn't work like
yours?

That's not how I think of
you.

                Then why did you lie to me??

I take deep breaths to try to calm my heart.

I wish I didn't. I promise I
will NEVER do it again. Not
even to save your life.

                That's another lie! You
                expect me to believe you'd
                stand there and let me jump
                off a bridge?

No. I'd grab your hand and
not let go. But I won't lie or
trick you again.

                What if you think I'm having
                an episode when I'm not? I
                don't see how this can work.
                I'll never know when you
                might be trying to trap me.

I will NEVER do it again no
matter what I think. I regret
it now more than anything.
Please give me another
chance.

My eyes itch. I type:

                I have to go.

Please don't give up on me.

I want to switch off my phone now except Mom made me promise not to. I put it on Do Not Disturb to leave it on but stop it from telling me if anyone calls or texts.

Even if I were like everybody else, I think I'd still be very mixed right now.

TWENTY-EIGHT

Hamster is *RUNNING*

Hummingbird is *FLYING*

Hammerhead is *SLOGGING*

Hanniganimal is *CRASHING / MIXED*

HJ stays home for Friday Night Binge. She and Mom sit on either side of me on the sofa and fail to get me to talk for the first hour. Now we're just watching the TV, though I'm not paying attention and don't know what's on anymore.

I can't stop thinking, about lots of things, everything, from today, last year, years ago, even things that haven't happened yet but probably will. I feel the signs of stress pushing me off balance, like before I ran to the bridge, and I know I'm crumbling again. Dr. Jordan helped me learn to recognize this so I could try to do something about it before I lose control, and I really should take an Ativan, or two or three, to shut it all down...but part of me resists. I should only take meds to help, not to hide, and I have this growing belief that I'm close to discovering an important truth if I can just let myself think about these things I've been avoiding for so long.

Dr. Jordan keeps telling me to talk about everything with my real doctor, and Dr. Oswald says talking about things will help, too, but it was Dr. Dharni who got under my skin yesterday in Group. He said not thinking about trauma is like a dog licking a sore on its leg. It might seem like keeping something painful out of your mind is protecting you, but you're actually making it worse, preventing it from healing.

Maybe I was just vulnerable in the hospital, but it was the first time I wondered if my ability to keep myself from thinking about something isn't a superpower at all. I've always thought I had the strength to avoid thinking about painful things. What if I actually *can't* think about them because I *lack* the strength?

I grab my phone and open the picture I took on the bridge. The letters scratched on the gray concrete look different when isolated on the screen, out of their environment. Here it looks more like a part of a tombstone. That's what it is, in a way... except... it's not just for Nolan....

It's clear to me now why I go to the track and watch the long jumpers. It's the closest I can come to visiting Nolan's grave. Only I've been doing it most every day before school for over a year. That's not paying respects, or remembering. It's not saying good-bye.

I need to say good-bye.

———

Dr. Jordan told me everyone with bipolar disorder is different—endless variations of moods, emotions, intensity, frequency, reactions, episodes, delusions, breakdowns—but even so, according to him, I'm unusual. A lot of people have it much worse, he said, though he also likes to say I have my moments. In all his years of practice, he says, he never met anyone who cycled as fast as me without getting angry. Just lucky, I guess.

Not entirely luck. Something about it must run in the family. HJ doesn't have rage fits, either, though she can get dark and moody, especially on her bad mornings. Thankfully she's learned to isolate herself or keep her mouth shut till it passes. Nolan only got irrationally angry occasionally. When he did, I would hide for a while. I didn't take it personally. It was just a state of mind, like being hungry. I came back when he calmed down.

My family definitely got dealt shitty cards, but something we have going for us is we've never wanted to hurt ourselves. No matter how depressed we get, how hopeless and pointless everything seems, including breathing, we want to keep on going. Even in mixed states, which HJ doesn't get like Nolan and me, I've never wanted to do anything permanent or fatal. Neither did Nolan. I know it.

Dr. Jordan also said the suicide rate would be even higher except the desire to leave this world often comes with a lack of desire to do anything, including going to the effort of killing oneself. Is that irony? I just know all this adds up to why they're so worried I'll end up like Nolan.

It's this dysphoric mania thing, where severe depression is mixed with a powerful energy and compulsion to act. For people who feel it, and who want to kill themselves, or are just overwhelmed by everything, it's the worst possible combination. I've tried to explain to Dr. Jordan that for people who *don't* want to commit suicide, like Nolan and me, it's not dangerous. It's just extremely unpleasant till it goes away. But he doesn't believe me and keeps saying I have to be careful.

I wish there were a way to get people to understand that treating me different than everyone else makes things worse, not better.

———

I should take some Ativan now that I've sorted things out but I can't get myself off the sofa. Mom keeps asking what I want to watch until I finally choose a wildlife documentary. I hope a soothing British accent will calm me down but it doesn't even hold all my attention so I also mess with my phone to burn off extra energy and brain cycles.

I'm not ready to read all the messages on my phone from when I was in the hospital, yet having them hang over my head is making me anxious. I see one from Connor, a couple from Declan, lots from Holly, and the most from Zumi, a lot of variations of "Get well soon!" They don't understand that I'm never going to get well.

"Mel?" Mom says. "Baby? Do you need anything?"

I shake my head. I do need something, but she can't give it to me.

She wipes both of my cheeks with her thumb. "You sure you're okay?"

"No, Mom. I'm not okay. But it is what it is."

This is about more than Nolan. I need to say good-bye to everyone. Not the big good-bye. Just go back to my old life of refusing Holly's rides, doing Chemistry homework with Declan, not talking to Zumi or Connor, hanging out every day at the Silver Sands Suites, plus tell David we'll never have that official first date. I need to end the drama and go back to how things were.

I stand up. "I'm going to bed."

"This early?" Mom says. "Are you sleepy?"

"No." I turn to HJ and say, "Maybe you can explain it to her."

HJ frowns.

"Sorry," I say to both of them. "Maybe I need to take something. Some Ativan. I'll see you tomorrow."

I don't take any pills. I'll need my energy. Now that I know what I need to do, I can't put it off any longer or I'll be back in the hospital by Monday—I can feel it.

I can't say good-bye to Nolan here. We left him behind when we moved. To do it right, I have to go back. As soon as possible. Alone.

Out in the other room the TV is still on but I hear Mom and HJ talking quietly. They don't shut the TV and lights off till midnight, which is late for Mom and early for HJ. By the time the house is settled, I'm even more wound up from forcing myself to stay still this long. It feels like my entire body is made of bees.

I dress in layers. Then I quietly make up my bed with extra blankets under the comforter to look like I'm in my usual cocoon. If I can get out without making a sound, no one will know I'm gone till morning. I can be a hundred miles away by then, which is perfect since that's how far I need to go. One hundred and nine, to be exact.

I had no idea when I put my bike in the garage that I'd be taking it out again only a few hours later. I pull the red handle on the big door, slowly ease it up manually, roll my bike outside, and then carefully lower the door again. I'm finally bundled, on my bike, ready to go, with my route mapped on my phone to give me directions, when I remember something.

I slip back into the house. On the top shelf of my closet, pushed against the back wall behind a box of old books, is a rolled-up gray shirt. It wasn't one of Nolan's favorites—just one I didn't think anyone would miss.

I fish it out and unroll it partway to reveal the thin paperback book of jokes Nolan bought for us at the stationery store on his last day. I slide it into my pants pocket. Then I unroll the shirt the rest of the way and catch the sparkly plywood Magic Wand before it falls.

TWENTY-NINE

Hamster is *Running*

Hummingbird is *Speeding*

Hammerhead is *Slogging*

Hanniganimal is *Crashing / Mixed*

The directions get convoluted—sometimes on bike trails, other times through city areas—to avoid freeways. The moon, half lit, half dark, rises higher and higher ahead. It doesn't shine bright enough to see where I'm going, but the bike headlight is strong.

After climbing uphill from the coast, the way is mostly flat to and across the Dumbarton Bridge to the East Bay. After Fremont starts the slow steady climb, up through Pleasanton, Livermore, and downhill through Tracy. With twenty miles still to go, the moon is high and the eastern sky starts getting pink.

I'm exhausted yet still not tired. My muscles burn but don't weaken. I'm trembling though it's unclear how much is from exertion and how much is from the fact that I've been ice cold for hours. I thought I'd have to make bathroom stops by now but I haven't felt the need. I haven't stopped pedaling once, not for red lights, not for traffic, not for anything. I'm making much better time than the map predicted. Maybe my real superpower is cycling.

The sun rises as I reach my first destination. I park at the bike racks in front of my old middle school. I also put away my phone. I won't need directions from here.

I frame my eyes with both hands and peer into the window of my old eighth-grade classroom. It looks very different, yet some things are the same. It still says MS. MALIK'S MENAGERIE over a bulletin board with photos of her current students. There's still a poster over the door to the hallway, a close-up of a woman's eye with a caption: "Who are you when no one is watching?"

Hanging by the door to the hall are two slats of dark wood with painted white letters: BOYS and GIRLS. They must have gotten rid of the old boys' Magic Wand hall pass when I didn't bring back the girls'.

I stretch for a minute and then continue riding down to the golf course trail. It's similar to the beach trail back home, my newer home, except it runs alongside golf links instead of the Pacific.

The Healthee Hut is still here, which I think is miraculous. On a Saturday it won't open for a few more hours. Sandy Park looks about the same except the swing set, slide, and playhouse all seem smaller than I remember.

The vacant lot behind the police station got paved over

since we were here. There are trailers parked on it with police badges painted on the sides. I keep pedaling.

The stationery store is out of business, with a huge FOR LEASE sign in its window. Inside it's completely empty, stripped down to unpainted drywall. I pull the now-mangled joke book out of my back pocket. It falls open naturally, to a page toward the middle, the page it's been opened to the most.

MODERN PSYCHIATRY

Q: Why didn't the psychiatrist believe anything his patients said?

A: Because they were all lying on his couch!

Q: Why did the psychiatrist use the spatula to flip burgers at the Bar-B-Que?

A: To avoid a slip of the tongs!

Back when Nolan bought it we found every page hilarious. I can't believe I understood half these jokes then. Now that I do, they're not laugh-out-loud funny. I want to go back to that time, to understand what we were thinking. How we felt.

I pedal through town. It's quiet except for the few people who need to work Saturday mornings and some old people who don't but are up anyway, out hunting up breakfast, looking for news still printed on paper, or taking slow walks.

I park at the bank in the same racks as the time Nolan and I came. It's the right building but I don't know if it's the same bank. Doesn't matter. It's closed today. That's fine. I'm not going inside.

Three years ago we did.

Ready to see something awesome? Bring your Magic Wand. You're gonna love this.

I didn't. I loved everything that day up to this point, when he led me through the glass doors in front and I saw the intense artificial light flickering hotly in his eyes. I didn't love anything for a long time after.

I worried the photos I saw online earlier were old and the fire escape would be gone. It's still here, around the side, though out of reach. I wasn't sure how I'd deal with that and figured I'd work out something when I got here.

A dumpster at the far end of the alley has wheels. Crappy wheels. Rusty. But it moves. Slowly.

The bottom of the fire-escape drop ladder is still a few feet out of reach. I climb back down and open the dumpster to look for a box or anything else to stand on. I see the answer right away: a beat-up umbrella, the classic black kind with a hook for a handle. This clinches it. I'm meant to get to the roof today.

———

"We'll get in trouble!" I say after the elevator doors close.

"You never get in trouble. Everything's always my fault."

"Let's go. The security guard was watching us. I think he was picking up the phone."

"You haven't seen the awesomeness yet! If they catch us they won't throw us in jail. They'll just tell us to leave."

Nolan bounces on his toes, making me nervous. He's really worked up and not looking at me much anymore. To get his attention, I say, "Where are we going?"

"All the way!"

The elevator goes to the top and stops on the seventh floor. Nolan leads me down a hall of closed wooden doors, through a big steel door, up some concrete steps, out another steel door, and into the sun. I can't imagine how he ever came to find whatever he wants to show me.

It's windy. Under our feet is loose gravel. The wall around the roof is only a foot high. It's obvious people aren't supposed to be up here. Not only for those reasons, but for a much bigger one.

There's a large skylight before us, maybe ten feet wide but very long, almost enough to cut the entire roof in half. Instead of being a flat grid of square panes, it's three long rows of dozens of glass pyramids sticking up, each about a foot tall. It's pretty, but it also looks like a hazard in a video game, an obstacle to jump over where you lose a life if you touch any part of it.

"My metalworking class came here to see this and I saw they didn't have to unlock any of the doors on the way up. Come look!"

He trots to the edge of the skylight. I walk slowly over and stop a few feet away, craning my neck to look. Even from here I can see how the space under the skylight goes all the way down to the ground.

"Come closer," Nolan says. "It's safe." He leans out and bends over to plant a hand on one of the glass pyramids. "See? It's solid. Good metalwork."

"Wow," I say. "Cool. Amazing. Awesome. Okay, let's go."

"That's not the awesome part! Stand over there." He points to a spot uncomfortably close to the edge of the roof.

"Why?"

"It's the best place to see."

"The wind will blow me off!"

"It won't. Okay, fine, come on..."

He walks me over to the far side of the roof. It takes a minute to go all the way to the front of the building, to get around the skylight, and then back to the middle of the other side again. He stands me in front of a fire escape. I grab its railing.

"There, now the wind's pushing you toward the building. Wait here."

"Where are you going!"

"Back to the other side."

He trots all the way around the skylight again to the far stairwell where we first emerged, bouncing on his feet way more than necessary. Maybe he wants to show me something about the glass pyramids, like the sun shining through them to make rainbows.

"Don't stand so close to the edge!" I shout.

"It's fine!" He puts his right foot back against the short wall, as if to push off from it. He crouches. "Okay, wave your Magic Wand!"

Somehow I knew, but I didn't want to believe it....

"You're not going to jump it, right?!"

He grins, laces his fingers together, cracks his knuckles, and he bends his neck to crack that, too.

"Piece of cake! Come on, wave your wand!"

"No way! Let's go! Come on! The guard's coming—I can hear him!"

I can't really, but I wish I could and I don't know what else to say. Nolan's too far away to reach. I wouldn't be any match for him anyway. Besides, he must be teasing. He won't really do this.

"C'mon!" I yell. "Let's go!"

He drops his head and his arms to dangle loosely. "All right, fine, I'm coming!"

Phew.

Nolan launches forward and runs straight toward me....

"NO!"

His third step slips in the gravel—he recovers and keeps sprinting....

"STOP!"

He jumps, grinning....

The toe of his trailing foot brushes the top of the first glass pyramid, just enough to tip him forward, arms spinning wildly....

It's not over quickly. There's no mercy in it. He crashes down heavily on the skylight, his knees punching through separate panes of glass, knocking him sideways as some pyramids shatter and *others stay intact. Nolan tangles up in broken glass and metal rods, scrabbling desperately to grab something, anything, but everything he touches is jagged and sharp. His pained, contorted face is lined with bloody cuts—*

"NOLAN!"

The entire framework collapses and he's gone.

THIRTY

Hamster is *Running*

Hummingbird is *Flying*

Hammerhead is *Slogging*

Hanniganimal is *Crashing / Mixed*

The skylight looks the same, rebuilt to match the antique original. Like it never happened.

I've lost track of time. I don't remember walking around to the far side of the roof where Nolan started his run. I don't remember sitting, or making this mound of gravel for the Magic Wand to stand up in. I don't remember starting to cry. I came to say good-bye, which meant letting Nolan all the way in, and this is why I never do that. I lose my mind every time.

His doctor called it subintentional suicide. That's when you take life-threatening risks to fool yourself into committing suicide without admitting it. It's why Sofia got locked up for mixing a bunch of pills without going full overdose. It'll take her a while to convince them she wasn't subconsciously trying to exit through the roof.

They said Nolan was having an episode of dysphoric mania, but I know he wasn't. He was showing no signs of darkness. He was just excited. He wasn't trying to leave this world, subintentionally or otherwise. He was trying to live in it as completely as possible. It's a critical difference. Night and day, really.

Mom yelled at Aunt Joan that meds were keeping me from ending up like Nolan, but I was the only one with him at the end, so how could she know? Except it makes sense, now that I let myself think about it. Why *wouldn't* I end up like him? My symptoms hadn't come in a big way yet, but he talked as if he knew they would. We were two of a kind, he'd said. No one understands us, or knows what it's like to be us, or will ever treat us like other people. We'll always be "special" and get "handled" so we had to stick together.

The truth is, the skylight only *looks* scary. I watch people jump this far all the time before school. I'm pretty sure I jumped farther myself with bloody bare feet. Nolan was just goofing off too much. He slipped but didn't go back to start again. He didn't aim between the pyramids well enough. And he jumped into the wind. It was just an accident. Bipolar disorder had nothing to do with it. Nolan died because he was a jackass.

But I'm not. I don't clown around. I take my meds. Everyone thinks they have to keep me under a microscope since I got built with the same broken parts as Nolan, but we're not the same in the ways that killed him…and now, thinking about this, I know how to prove it.…

It's actually pretty simple. I'm surprised I never thought of it before. The key to everything is that the jump is *dangerous*, yes, but not *impossible*. Not even that hard, as long as you take it seriously. All I have to do is make the jump myself. That will prove it's possible, and *that* will prove Nolan wasn't delusional to think he could make it, and it will also prove I'm not the jackass my brother was. They'll see that I'm not someone to worry about.

All I need to do is prop up my phone on the short wall and record myself making the jump to show everyone later. But first I need to stop crying. Then I can finish what Nolan started and say good-bye—

Rattling metal startles me. I stumble to my feet.

David appears on the other side of the roof, from the fire escape.

I put up both hands. "Stay back!"

"Mel!" David calls. "Don't jump!"

I'm standing near the edge of the building so of course he thinks I'm here to jump off. I'll always be a ticking time bomb to everyone. Seeing the fear on David's face reminds me how I was right to hide my diagnosis. The ache in my chest is real, physical.... How can my heart keep breaking again and again? It's like a cat with nine lives, only that's another way of saying nine deaths....

"Come away from the edge," David says. "Please."

If it weren't for the skylight between us, I'm sure he'd have tackled me already.

"What are you doing here?" I ask.

"I was worried about you," he says. "It was too early to call. So I...I used the tracker to...you know...make sure you were home and safe. Then I saw you heading out here. I tried texting and calling. Why didn't you answer?"

I remember now: Do Not Disturb mode.

David says, "I thought you might be coming to visit the cemetery and I wanted to come with you—"

"What?!" I take a step, mostly to keep from falling over. "How...?"

"Joan told me about Nolan."

Hurricane Joan. Wreaking havoc.

"Mel, please come away from the edge—"

"*God!* I'm not here to jump off the roof!"

"Promise me."

"Fine, I promise I won't jump...off the roof."

He squints. "Promise you won't jump *anywhere*."

I guess Aunt Joan told him everything.

"Just...leave, okay?" I say. "Just leave me alone."

"No. Promise me you won't jump the skylight."

"It's...It's...not impossible...and he thought he could make it—" A sob interrupts me.

"I believe you," David says. "I'm sure it was just an accident—"

"I know! I'll show you!"

"No!" David takes a quick step forward.

"I can do it!"

"Not after riding your bike all night! Look at you...you're a mess! You couldn't jump over a crack in the sidewalk. Let's go home and later we can—"

264

"No! You'll make it so I can't come back!"

"Mel...you won't *want* to come back. Not when you're thinking straight again."

"You don't know what I'm thinking." Everything's blurring and I wipe my eyes. "When I make it, you'll see I'm not going to end up like him, and then everyone can stop worrying."

"Look at me," David says, but I can't. "If you do this, even if you *don't* fall—and you definitely *will*—it'll make people think you *are* going to end up like Nolan. What'll make you the same is *trying*. The only way to prove you're different is to *not try*."

"You're wrong," I say. But I'm getting confused...he's trying to confuse me....

I wipe my eyes again and see the Magic Wand in its mound of gravel. I pick it up. Nolan had told me to wave it, but I didn't. Maybe I should have.

"Come on, Mel. Let's go somewhere and talk about this."

I know what that means. They'll seal or lock the fire escape, weld the doors shut, who knows, but they won't let me back up here again. It's now or never.

I touch the far wall with my heel, brace my foot against it, lean down—

"Mel, wait! I'll do it!"

David drops to one knee and starts tightening his shoelaces.

This startles me for some reason.

"You just want proof that it's possible?" he says. "So I'll prove it and we can go."

265

I peer at him. Is this a trick?

"It doesn't have to be you," he says. "Right?"

I'm really confused. I don't know if he's right or not.

He switches to the laces of his other shoe and says, "You're so tired you can't even stand straight without wobbling. I know I can make it if I'm careful and don't slip, but I won't lie; this sort of stunt often ends badly on YouTube. I just don't see any other way to stop you."

I'm losing track of the details but one thing is clear: He's really going to do this—

My heart stops.

I see it now. I understand.

Maybe this is how it was with Nolan. I don't want to die, and I know there's a chance I could fall, but somehow this doesn't frighten me....

Yet watching David now...it changes everything. Seeing him about to do this instead of me...*for* me...I'm suddenly terrified.

He isn't trying to patronize me. Or handle me. Or pat me on the head and go on with his business. He's really trying to help. Even if it kills him.

"David, don't!"

He looks up. "Why?"

"It's...it's too dangerous! It's not worth it. It doesn't matter. Let's just go, okay?"

"No," he says and returns to his laces. "I can't tell if you really believe that. Maybe you're only saying it to keep me from jumping—"

He stops and stares at me. Then he rocks back and sits in the gravel.

"This is how *you* feel," he says. "Isn't it?"

David watches me. Like he wants an answer. But I don't know what he means.

"You know," he says, "when people try to talk you out of doing something? And you don't know whether or not they're lying, just saying anything to get you to stop?"

I nod.

He looks down at his shoes for a moment, then back at me. "I will *never* do it to you again, Mel. I *swear.*"

I believe him.

He says, "Promise you'll never do it to me?"

I nod again.

"All right. So if we leave, are you going to want to come back alone later and try this?"

I open my mouth to reply, but what's the truth? I want to say *no*, but I'm not sure that's—

"Thanks for not lying," he says grimly. He stands. "I'm coming over."

"No, don't!"

He bends down and plants a foot against the short wall.

"I...I..." I want so badly to tell him I'll never come back, anything to stop him from jumping, even if it's a lie.... This must be how he feels, and it's horrible.

And now I'm reliving my worst memory, standing help-less on this roof, about to watch someone do something ridic-ulously dangerous, utterly pointless, and probably fatal. And like last time, there's nothing I can do to stop it.

Yet I don't feel helpless despair this time. I feel...I'm not sure what....

David crouches and positions his hands on the gravel like a sprinter. Does he do track and field at his school? I don't even know.

"Don't do it!" I shout. "I don't want you to!"

He ignores me and settles himself. Nolan ignored me, too. And not just that once, but also other times. It was infuriating.

David launches himself and sprints toward me.

I hurl the Magic Wand across the roof and yell, *"If you jump I'll never talk to you again!"*

He skids to a stop, spraying gravel. I don't know if it was because I shouted or to dodge the Magic Wand.

I hold out my hands, palms down. "See? I'm not shaking. It's not a lie—I'll *never* speak to you again!"

He watches me. Then he says, "I believe you, but I can live with it if it keeps you from falling down this hole later." He shakes his head. "You can't talk me out of this."

"Yes I can." I squat and push my right foot against the short wall, ready to run. "I'll do whatever you do. If it's okay for you, it's okay for me."

"Mel? What—"

"If you jump, I'll jump. If you leave, I'll leave. Either we do this or we don't. It's up to you."

Now *he* looks confused.

He says, "If we leave, how do I know you won't come back later—"

"You don't. Maybe I will. You can't control me."

"That's not what I want."

"I don't know for sure what I'm going to do tomorrow," I say, "so I can't promise anything. Neither can you—"

268

"Mel, I promise you, one hundred percent; I'll never try to jump over this death trap as long as you promise, too."

"Well, I can't. If that's too much for you, I'm sorry."

He walks over a few steps and picks up the Magic Wand. He stands there looking at it. I'm not sure from here but maybe he's smiling? I can't imagine why.

"Come on, David. Are we doing this or not? I'm getting hungry."

He chuckles, spinning the Magic Wand in his hand, looking at it.

"Quit stalling. I want breakfast. With extra bacon."

He walks toward me. After a few steps, he says, "I thought you were going to do whatever I did."

I walk forward, too. We stop ten feet apart, the skylight between us. He pivots and walks along his edge, and I walk along mine. By the time we reach the far end, our steps are synchronized.

We round the skylight and walk toward each other. He holds out his arms. I do the same. We hug.

He squeezes me and whispers, "Please don't come here again."

"I'll do my best, but no promises. You might have heard; sometimes I don't think straight."

He snorts. "That's an understatement."

I pull back. "Are...are you making fun of me?"

He raises his eyebrows. "Too soon?"

"No!" I hug him again, tightly. "Not too soon."

We head for the fire escape. Halfway there I notice we're holding hands. At the ladder, he raises the Magic Wand.

"Here, you dropped this." He shrugs. "Sort of."

I take it and slide it into my back pocket, star down, with the joke book.

"You know," I say, "I didn't come to jump. It's not something I've been thinking about. It never occurred to me till I got here. I just came to say good-bye."

"So did you?"

"No. I thought this would be the right place to do it, but it's not."

THIRTY-ONE

Hamster is *Running*

Hummingbird is *Flying*

Hammerhead is *Cruising*

Hanniganimal is *Up!*

David and I walk together along the western railing of the Golden Gate Bridge, watching the Saturday sailboats tacking back and forth across the mouth of the bay. I haven't told him why we're here. When he asked where I wanted to go on our first official date, I said I wanted to show him something on the bridge. We could decide where to go from there.

When we reach the south tower, I glance down and see the letters scratched in the concrete but don't say anything yet. Instead I stand at the rail and hold out the Magic Wand, letting it bounce around in the wind.

My seventeenth birthday party was at the Silver Sands last night—family and friends mixing with the residents—and I'm sure Judith is still regretting it. Not only had the Beach-front Lounge never held so many teenagers at once, it had never had a karaoke machine in it. Connor and David escaped

271

the mic, but not Declan. Holly dragged him up with her more than once, though I don't know if her whispers to him were threats or promises.

Zumi, of course, was unstoppable. In a night of unforgettable moments, the high point had to be Zumi and Mr. Terrance Knight singing Sonny and Cher's "I Got You Babe" to each other.

On the bridge, David and I look out over the water in comfortable silence. The traffic is pretty loud, actually, but it seems farther away than it really is.

I get a text from Holly.

Movie Roulette tonight?

I let David see it. I hold the phone so he can watch me type.

Can't. Busy.

Is that so? Bring him along. ;)

Next time. Have fun! Don't make any little girls cry!

You too! Later. :)

David leans on the rail next to me. "How far we going?"

He doesn't mess around. Straight to the point. I like it.

I pivot and point down. "Nolan did that. When he was eleven and I was eight."

David squats. "*N, A, H.* Is this why you were here when I...picked you up before? To look at this again?"

I nod.

"Aaron? Alex?"

"Paul. Nolan Paul Hannigan."

David looks puzzled. I take a deep breath. I want to do this, but...

"Those aren't his initials. They're both of ours. *His* first name, *my* first name, and our last name." I swallow. "Mel is... just a nickname."

"But..." He stops. Then he stands. "What's your real name?"

"I want you to know, but..."

David steps closer.

"When I was born, Nolan couldn't pronounce my whole name. Just the *Mel* part, and he couldn't even say that right. So everyone called me Mel. Later, he could say my whole name and sometimes did, but everyone had been calling me Mel for so long.... He started out being the only one who couldn't say my real name, then he became the only one who ever did."

I pause. David takes my hands.

"Then, after the accident, I couldn't hear it without losing my mind. Grandma Cece told the residents to never say it. I haven't told anyone, not even Zumi. I haven't gotten a driver's license because... you know. Only Connor found out, him and his damn Web searches. He kept it secret for me."

"Connor's a good guy," David says. "All your friends are great. Even Zumi."

"Yeah, even Zumi." I smile. "Anyway, I want you to know it, but I'm not ready to hear it out loud. Soon, I hope."

"I won't say it till you tell me it's okay."

I nod but don't say anything.

"I know it's got *M-E-L* in it," he prompts. "And it starts with an *A*. . . ."

"And it ends with an *A*. And there's an *I* in it. That's all."

"I like it," he says. "I hope I get to call you that soon."

"Me too. You'll be the first to know."

"I feel like you've given me something," he says. "I hope you weren't secretly hoping I'd get you a birthday present. You made me promise not to."

"I don't like getting stuff."

"Doesn't seem fair."

"I said no presents. I didn't say you couldn't give me anything."

I tip my nose up a little. He leans forward and kisses me.

It's every bit as wonderful as the first time. And the second. And all the other times last week. I lost count.

Then he pulls back and says, "All right, I can't take it anymore. This is a new hoodie, isn't it?"

"How would you know? You haven't seen half my clothes."

He reaches behind me, peels something off my back, and dangles it. It's a long thin clear sticker covered in black *M*s.

"Oh! Oops."

"I think someone broke your 'no presents' rule last night."

"What? No! I refuse them if anyone tries."

"Really?" he says. "Even if it's someone who *also* wears black hoodies with big white letters?"

I pull on the hem to flatten it out. It says: BORN TO BE WILD.

"This wasn't a birthday present. It's just friends buying stuff for friends. Getting it at the party was a coincidence."

"What if I give you something, just by coincidence?"

"Too late now—I'm wise to you. I said anyone who couldn't resist giving me something could make me a card. You had your chance. Too late now."

He holds out an envelope.

I snatch it from him and open it. On the front of the card is a watercolor of a woman in an old-time dress riding a bicycle. Inside it's blank except for David's handwriting.

Happy Birthday, Mel.

Looking forward to the other 90%.

David

"Thank you." I kiss him. "Same to you."

I carefully set the Magic Wand down at the base of the tower, next to Nolan's marks. Then I grab David's hand. "Come on."

"Where to?"

I point ahead to the north tower.

"Let's start there."

ACKNOWLEDGMENTS

Thanks to my agent, Jennifer Weltz at JVNLA, for being such a wonderful navigator in all things, providing kind honesty at every turn while enduring my tendency to overthink everything. And to our UK agent, Nicola Barr at Greene & Heaton, for her excellent representation.

Thanks to my editor at LBYR, Pam Gruber, for diving deep into Mel's world with me to find the story I wanted to tell and bring it to the surface. To copy chief Jen Graham, production editor Annie McDonnell, copyeditor Sarah Chassé, and proofreader Jodie Lowe for smoothing out the rough spots. To Maggie Edkins for the amazing book design and brilliant cover! To Kristina Aven, Emilie Polster, Jenny Choy, Stefanie Hoffman, Jennifer McClelland-Smith, and Jane Lee for their excellent PR. To Alvina Ling, Farrin Jacobs, Shawn Foster,

Victoria Stapleton, and Leslie Shumate, plus Megan Tingley, Andrew Smith, and Carol Scatorchio, for putting their faith in Mel Hannigan. And to Ruth Alltimes of HCUK for coming in early to help us to the finish.

Thanks especially to the many people who share their experiences in mental health with the world and me personally. Without such open and honest accounts, true understanding would not be possible, and certainly this book would not have been.

Belated thanks to the writers I met early in my career who inspired me: Zina Yee for showing me the importance of details and consistency, Michael Humes for his examples of strength and integrity, David Luoto for his relentless out-of-left-field creativity, and Marti and Bridget McKenna for so much writing hospitality.

And special thanks to my family for accepting and loving me for who I truly am. Especially Susan, my number one fan; Shannon, for keeping me stepping right; and Rachel, for giving me back my confidence whenever I lost it in the house somewhere.

HANNIGANIMAL TRACKING
Thursday, March 19 – Saturday, April 11

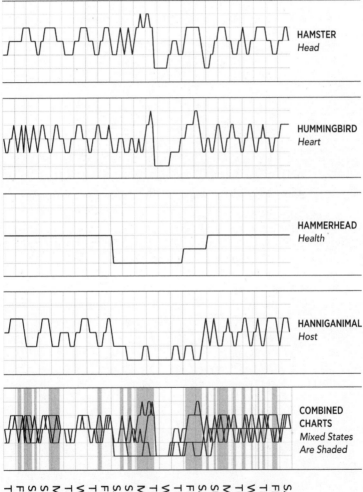

HAMSTER
Head

HUMMINGBIRD
Heart

HAMMERHEAD
Health

HANNIGANIMAL
Host

COMBINED
CHARTS
*Mixed States
Are Shaded*

THU
FRI
SAT
SUN
MON
TUE
WED
THU
FRI
SAT*
SUN**
MON***
TUE****
WED*****
THU
FRI
SAT
SUN
MON
TUE
WED
THU
FRI
SAT